THEY RISE

HUNTER SHEA

SEVERED PRESS
HOBART TASMANIA

THEY RISE

Copyright © 2015 Hunter Shea
Copyright © 2015 by Severed Press

WWW.SEVEREDPRESS.COM

ISBN: 978-1-925342-70-3

For all lovers of a good yarn from the sea – especially you, Erin!

ONE

"You want a beer, Richie?"

"Ed, it's only nine o'clock. I just finished my coffee."

It was still a bit on the chilly side out on the water. A steady breeze sweeping from the east gently rocked the party fishing boat, white caps dominating the Atlantic Ocean's undulating surface.

"Okee dokee, just checking." Eddie Dawson lifted the lid of his old, battered Coleman cooler, nestling the can of Labatt Blue next to its five brethren in the ice. Eddie had never had a beer in his seventy plus years, but he made sure to always have it on hand when he went fishing. His brother, Richie, liked a beer every now and then, especially Labatt, which is why he'd bought a sixer the night before.

"Hey, Ed, I'll take one," Al West said. He hung over the railing, staring at his taut line as if he could will a snapper or grouper to bite. What remained of his gray hair was blown wild by the wind.

"Sure, Al, sure." He handed his old friend a can, making sure to wipe the condensation off with his shirt. He didn't want it to slip from Al's arthritic hand.

Taking a bite of chocolate from the bar he had in his jacket pocket, Eddie reached over to get his fishing pole back from Richie. He gave it a few tugs, felt nothing on the other end. Some days were like this. They'd been out on the water for two hours and he'd only heard one person call for the mate to bring the net.

If there were no fish to eat tonight, Eddie figured he'd go to the diner. Thursday was navy bean soup night. He loved his navy bean soup. That and some steak fries with a coffee would do him just fine.

"Did you schedule your echocardiogram?" Richie asked. Eddie's older brother by four years looked a lot like Frank Sinatra in his later years, minus the hairpiece. His pale blue eyes watered from the wind.

"It slipped my mind," Eddie said, staring off into the horizon. "I'll call tomorrow."

"You want me to call for you?"

"No, no, I'll do it. I just forgot about it."

His brother turned to him. "Ed, you can't forget these things. Hearts like ours would have stopped a long time ago if we didn't stay on top of things."

He was right. Their genetic pool was overflowing with every heart condition known to man. Sometimes, Eddie was glad he'd never had kids so he couldn't pass it down to another generation.

"That's an easy one," Al said, taking a long sip from his beer. "I'll take that over my annual colonoscopy any day. And why are those colonoscopy nurses always young and pretty? It's bad enough that I'm older than most of their grandfathers. They have to see my keister at its worst, too?" He guffawed, tapping the shoulder of the man next to him to share in the fun. Al was like that, loud and working hard to be the funniest man in the room, or, in this case, on the boat.

"I won't forget...tomorrow," Eddie said, offering Richie a square of chocolate.

"Mary or I can do it for you." He took the chocolate, popped it whole in his mouth.

And that was Richie, still treating him like a kid brother even though they were a combined age of one hundred fifty-three.

Eddie was about to reassure him that he could do it all by himself, while secretly wondering if he *would* remember twenty-four hours from now, when the rod jumped in his hands. The reel sang as a fish tugged on the line, dragging it under the boat.

"You got something there, Okee Dokee," Al said.

Most people called him Okee Dokee. The two dozen men on the boat, captain and mate only knew him as Okee Dokee. That was fine by him. Say something enough times, he guessed people identified you by it.

He tugged back, letting more of the line play out, trying to judge what he'd hooked by the weight and fight of the fish.

"Feels like a big one," he said.

"Let him wear himself out," Richie said, pulling his own line up in case Eddie needed help.

"You got him, just reel him in before he tangles up the lines on the other side," Al advised. He had taken his line out of the water too, reaching into the cooler for another beer.

"It's too early if it's a big one," Richie said.

"It's definitely not a grouper," Eddie said, the muscles in his forearms straining. In a way, he hoped it wasn't a big fish. The days of going out for big fish like tarpon, marlin, tilapia and even the occasional shark, the hours-long battles, were all behind him. It's why he preferred the party boats now, fishing for smaller fish with much less fight. The mind was willing, but the body was weak. It was just like his favorite line from *Dirty Harry* – "A man's got to know his limitations."

"Let me know if you need a rest," Richie said. "I can take over for a bit."

Eddie saw his brother slip one of his miniscule nitro pills under his tongue. No, he was definitely not handing this over to him, not if he was already having chest pains. These days, it didn't take much for Richie to hit the nitro.

"Hey Blondie, you might want to get your ass over here," Al shouted. Blondie was a tan mate with curly blond hair and the graceful gait of a kid who spent a lifetime on the water. He worked the party boats on days when he didn't have classes at Miami Dade College. The kid was tall and wiry and exceedingly good-natured, as well as perpetually shirtless. He came hopping over to their side of the boat, his flip-flops slapping against the bottoms of his feet.

"You got a good one, Okee Dokee?" he said.

Eddie nodded, giving a small laugh. "I sure do. Feels like a whopper."

The way his pole bent now, it looked about to snap in two.

"It sure as hell is," Blondie said. He ran to get a long pole with a hook on the end and the largest net they carried.

Now everyone was looking Eddie's way. The captain brought the engine to life, turning the boat so the line was no longer being pulled directly beneath it.

Maybe I won't be eating at the diner tonight, Eddie thought. Images of a hot cup of navy bean soup were replaced by the very real pain he was feeling in his arms and back.

"You're doing great, Ed," his brother said.

"Let's not make this an all day affair," Al cautioned with a chuckle. "I have a nap to take at noon."

The boat dipped violently as it was buffeted by a surge of rough waves. The line pulled tighter, and Eddie felt something give.

"I think I lost it," he said, grateful for the break in tension.

"Reel up some slack," Richie said. Blondie was on Eddie's left, staring into the water, waiting for his moment, if there would indeed be one now.

Eddie cranked the reel, yards of fishing line spooling back with ease. Whatever he'd hooked was most definitely gone. Other fishermen, all of them old and experienced, heard the quick and easy clicking of the reel and set about dropping their lines back in.

"Win some, lose some," Eddie said, smiling.

"Lose most," Al joked.

Suddenly, the line got heavy again.

"Wait," Eddie said, still bringing in some line, but slower now. Maybe another fish had grabbed hold of the hook. It had happened to him before.

"Keep it coming," Richie said, his hand on Eddie's shoulder. "At least you'll get something for your troubles."

Turning the reel faster, it was as if he were trying to catch up with the fish as it made a mad dash for the surface. What the hell had he hooked?

"I think I see it!" Blondie said, dipping the net in the water, close to Eddie's line. "Don't stop, Okee Dokee."

Eddie pulled, reeled some more, tugged on the pole, took in more slack. Oh, it was almost here. He could feel it.

"Christ, what the hell is that?" Al said, staring over the rail. Eddie didn't dare look. He had to concentrate on getting the fish near Blondie's net.

"Someone take my pole," Blondie said. The man next to him grabbed it so he could grip the net with two hands. "Just a little more, Okee."

Eddie heard wild thrashing. Blondie arched over the rail, sweat instantly streaming down the sides of his face. "Holy cow!" he exclaimed.

The other mate, the captain's son who was no older than sixteen, hustled over to help him bring it in.

Now looking down, Eddie saw a massive fish struggling in the green net. It was bigger than the green mesh could contain, but enough of it had been snagged to haul it on board.

"You ever see anything like it?" he said.

Richie shook his head. "I'll be jiggered. Leave it to you, Ed."

Both mates grunted and cursed, but managed to swing the net over the deck. Normally, this is where they'd jump in to remove the hook from the mouth of the fish.

Not this time.

At around six feet, the alien fish had what looked like a series of scales or plates on its face, with a pronounced dorsal fin. Its flesh was a mottled brown with streaks of gray. It gnashed at the net, its long tail whipping back and forth, struggling like a cornered bearcat. The violence of its struggles frayed the mesh until most of it was free.

"Hook it," someone said, meaning the mates should drive the point at the end of the pole into its head. The man holding the pole dropped it, stepping away from the creature.

"Eddie, don't get close!" Richie said, grabbing his arm.

"It looks like a goddamn steel-plated shark," Al said, steering clear from its thrashing tail.

Eddie was about to reach down for the pole, since Blondie and the kid were statues, eyes wide with stunned amazement, when he heard his brother groan.

Richie collapsed into Al, clutching his left shoulder.

No!

"Hold on, Richie, I'll get a pill," Eddie said, fumbling through his brother's pockets.

Blondie's scream stopped him cold.

The boy's forearm was a bloody mess.

"It stung him," someone said, and now there was panic as everyone trampled to the front of the boat. The captain shouted for the frightened men to calm down.

Blondie's eyes rolled up in his head and he collapsed next to the captive fish. His arm was beginning to swell, the flesh turning a diseased yellow.

Eddie found the pill case, jamming one under Richie's tongue. "My brother is having a heart attack!" he shouted, but no one heard.

All eyes were on the hulking fish and Blondie's rapidly rotting arm.

TWO

Brad Whitley awoke with a hell of a hangover, the film of last night's beer and cheap tequila shots thick on his tongue. Rolling over in bed, he found a thong tangled in the sheets.

"Hello?" he called out, praying there wouldn't be a reply.

To his relief, there was none. The hotel room's bathroom door was open and he could see by the mirror on the opposite wall that it was empty.

Maybe coming in last night hadn't been the best idea. Too many distractions in Miami, and none of the ones he preferred were good for him.

A bottle of warm Land Shark was on the bedside table. He considered drinking it just to shave some of the layers off his tongue, but thought better of it. The room spun when he got to his feet. He took it slow, shuffling to the bathroom to pee. When he was done, he turned on the cold water, tilting his open mouth under the faucet, lapping up as much as he could just the way his dog drank out of the kitchen sink.

You are a big, dumb animal.

Smoothing the prematurely graying hair at his temples with cold water, he noted how pink the old scar on his left cheek looked. The jagged line went to his temple, in stark relief to his pale face. His lean body was a patchwork of scars. All part of the job. Coral reefs, hooks and frightened big fish had a way of leaving their mark.

He suspected the owner of the thong was a stripper from the club he vaguely remembered stumbling into after hours spent at an open-air bar across from the beach. He allowed himself to exhale when he saw the used condom on the floor.

"At least you weren't a total moron."

He lay back on the bed, staring at the ceiling, then checked his watch.

Two hours to lie in misery before his appointment. He was going to make a hell of a first impression.

But it had been a long time since he'd been in the States. Who could begrudge him a little party time, especially down here where every woman looked like a super model, wearing just enough clothes to cover the good parts.

"I know who," he said. Talking out loud with no one around had become a disturbing habit. If it crept into his time in the company of others, he would seek help. "Everyone you're going to meet today."

He moaned, set the alarm for one hour, and tried to fall back to sleep.

The heavyset Hispanic man removed his cream Panama fedora, using it to fan his face. His thin mustache looked to be dyed black, in contrast to the thin, silver hair on the top of his head.

"You the marine biologist?" he said, eyeing him sitting at the table for two in the hotel's empty dining room.

"Ichthyologist," Brad said, sipping a Bloody Mary. It was spicy as hell, just what he needed.

"So you're not Brad Whitley? I'm sorry. I was sent to pick up this guy."

He motioned for the man to take the seat opposite him. "Marine biologist is a general term, like calling Tom Brady a football player when he's technically a quarterback. And you are?"

"Nestor Garza." He wiped a few beads of sweat from his upper lip with a starched handkerchief. "I'm with the Seaquarium."

"You can call me Whit." He tilted his glass toward the man. "I can order one if you like."

Nestor waved him off. "So what's an ichthyologist?"

"It's a fancy way of saying I study fish – cartilaginous fish to be exact. I try not to brag too much."

The man paused, looking deep into Whit's bloodshot eyes, wondering if he should laugh or not. Whit let him off the hook by smiling.

"So, you're my ride?" Whit said, polishing off the Bloody Mary.

"At your service."

"What do you do at the Seaquarium?"

"A little bit of everything. I'm a volunteer without any kind of special marine biology degree. I retired from the postal service a couple of years ago and couldn't see myself getting into gardening. So, now I help out wherever I can. Plus I get discounts for my family when they come to the aquarium. It makes grandpa the hero." His teeth were dazzling white, eyes shining like a proud patriarch.

Whit asked, "Have you seen it?"

"Seen what?"

"The fish. The one they pulled from that party boat."

Nestor shook his head. "Not yet. I was hoping I could today."

Whit rose from his chair, took a moment to let the spins clear from his head. "I'll make sure you do. Well, lead the way."

They rode in Nestor's air-conditioned Mazda, the morning sun searing Whit's eyes. He must have lost his sunglasses last night. He made a note to buy a new pair later. He pulled the visor down, shifting it to block the rays coming in the side window.

Nestor made some small talk, but not too much to tax Whit's dehydrated brain. He had a very slight Spanish accent and smiled a lot.

Whit removed a folded printout of the fish, the color photo not taken in the best light, but well enough to get his ass on a plane from Perth.

"Do you know if the man it stung is all right?" Whit asked.

Nestor's lips pulled tight. "He's still alive, but they had to remove his arm. I don't think he's doing too well."

They pulled into the Miami Seaquarium, Nestor parking in the lot reserved for employees. It had been decided that the aquarium was the best place to store the body, keeping it in conditions close to its actual environment.

Getting out of the car, Whit could already feel the humidity rising. Good. He liked it hot and sticky.

"Follow me," Nestor said with what looked to be an extra bounce in his step. He must be curious as hell about what's inside, Whit thought.

Whit followed him into the building, a semicircular stadium painted blue. It must be where they put on shows with whales or dolphins. Whit despised aquariums and zoos for very obvious reasons. He felt his shoulders tense as they stepped into the cool semi-darkness.

"The fish is in a salt water tank just around here," Nestor said, guiding him through the narrow hallway. They went through a swinging set of doors, entering a large, rectangular room dominated by what looked to be a 2,000-gallon fish tank on a platform. A few spare lights were on, but the tank itself was unlit.

For the first time since arriving in Miami, Whit felt a tingle of excitement in his lower back, hands and scalp.

A woman wearing a white lab coat, her blonde hair in a bun, glasses on the tip of her nose, stood next to the tank, fingers swiping along her tablet. She looked startled when they walked in.

"Dr. Whitley?" she said, tucking the tablet under her arm.

"Please, just Whit," he said, shaking her hand.

She was pretty, in a bookish kind of way. A little mascara, some lipstick, ditch the librarian bun…

Her grip was firm, all business.

"Dhalia Shields. I do consulting work for the aquarium while I'm getting my masters at U of M."

"I take it the catch of the day is in there," he said, nodding at the tank.

"At least until the end of the day," Dhalia said. "After that, the aquarium needs it back." Looking to Nestor, she said, "Thank you so much for bringing Mr. – ah, Whit – here. You think you can come back around five?"

Before Nestor could leave, Whit said, "Hold on. Might as well stay for the unveiling."

Nestor broke out in a big smile.

"All righty, why don't we hit the lights," Whit said.

Dhalia walked over to a small panel by the tank and flipped a switch. A half-dozen lights came to life, all of them focused on the interior of the tank.

What Whit saw took his breath away.

"It doesn't look real," Nestor said, taking a step back.

The enormous, mottled fish lay on its side, a cold, black eye glaring back at them. Its front dorsal fin had gone limp, the tip pointing at the bottom of the tank.

Whit rubbed his chin, his mind going from zero to a hundred in the blink of an eye. "That's because it's not supposed to be."

THREE

"I'm going to need to get this to Florida International University. It's close and they have a biology lab," Whit said, circling the tank like a shark. Passing Dhalia, he placed a hand on her shoulder. "Thank you for having the foresight to take it here."

"I've had the water chilled to slow decomposition. The captain of the fishing boat wanted to slice it open, I think throw it back into the ocean. He was pretty upset over what it had done to his mate."

"I can see why," Whit said. "Can you look up the number for the University's dean?"

No sooner had he said it than Dhalia was busy tapping on her tablet.

He bumped into a stunned Nestor.

"Do you know what it is?" Nestor said.

Whit took a deep breath. "I should. Been studying these ancient critters all my life, though I've never seen one quite like this. The largest one ever recorded was just about four feet. This guy is easily six."

"Your fish is so damn ugly," Nestor said, wiping at his face with the handkerchief again even though it was downright chilly in the room.

"I wouldn't exactly call it *my* fish. They're not the prettiest fish in the sea. People call them ghost sharks, though they're not sharks at all, despite a distant relation. What you're seeing here is a chimaera fish, one of the oldest fish in the ocean. They've been around for over 400 million years, longer even than sharks."

Nestor inched forward to take a closer look. "I can see why they've been around so long. That face alone would scare a Great White away."

The chimaera's face did appear to be made of plates of battle-scarred armor, the large eyes reflecting a sort of primordial sentience, completely at odds with the modern world. It was what had attracted Whit to them years ago. Chimaeras were, in essence, living dinosaurs.

Whit reached into the tank, fingers brushing against its cold flesh. "Trust me, a Great White wouldn't hesitate to make this guy a meal, despite his mug and size."

Dhalia, who had been on the phone, sidled up next to them. "The University is sending a truck over in a couple of hours. The dean seemed pretty excited."

"He should be," Whit said, restraining himself from getting in the water with the chimaera.

"She," Dhalia said.

"Huh?"

It has to be six and a half feet, at least. I can only imagine how much it weighs. Where have you been hiding?

"The dean is a she. Dr. Crane."

"Oh, yeah, sure." He vaguely remembered meeting a Dr. Crane at a convention some years ago. If he recalled correctly, she had a ribald sense of humor and sparkling, green eyes. They'd hit it off well, at least until his wife had dragged him away. According to her, they had work the next day and he was one drink away from making an ass of himself.

Little did she know, he'd had just enough to make an ass of himself.

"You want some alone time?" Dhalia asked, one eyebrow arched.

Whit caught her sarcasm.

"This shouldn't even be here," Whit said. "Not in this part of the Atlantic. And certainly not this big."

"I'm going to see it in my nightmares for the rest of my life," Nestor said.

"Be careful of the dorsal fin," Dhalia said. "Its sting almost killed a man."

Gently touching the base of the fin, Whit replied, "The venom would be delivered from the spine in front of the fin. I won't take any chances, but I'll stake my paycheck that whatever toxins it had are dormant now. Chimaera stings aren't supposed to be deadly to humans."

"This one's was pretty wicked," Dhalia reminded him.

He turned to Nestor. "Do you know what hospital they're keeping the mate?"

"I think he's at Baptist Hospital."

"Can you take me there and be back here before the University guys come to pick up handsome?"

"Won't be any traffic this time of day. Sure, no sweat."

Wiping his hand dry on his pants, Whit said, "Dhalia, if they get here before we return, please stall them. I want to travel with it when they take it to the university."

She nodded, pushing her pink-framed glasses to the bridge of her nose. "No worries. I'll let them know you called shotgun."

As they hurried to Nestor's car, Whit looked back to catch Dhalia's lingering gaze.

Gotta watch out for those librarian types.

He'd gotten himself in plenty of hot water with women like Dhalia before. No, this time around, his dancing partner was that hideous old fish back there.

FOUR

Suzanne Merriweather watched the tiny bubbles break the surface of the ocean. It was like floating atop a giant bottle of seltzer. Lowering the instruments into the water, she buried her nose in the collar of her shirt. The smell out here was not pleasant. The rank odor came courtesy of the fizzing, popping bubbles, releasing tiny bursts of methane into the air.

Two years ago, a major release of methane from the Pacific floor had caused the evacuation of two beach towns outside Los Angeles. People panicked, thinking a homegrown terrorist had released a deadly gas in the area. Her team had been called in to investigate and ultimately let the people know that they had nothing to fear.

Mother Nature must have had a good laugh over that one.

When she was done, she went back to the bridge.

The hydrographic survey vessel, called *Porpoise IV*, was a 150-foot long scientific craft donated seven years ago by the U.S. Navy to NOAA, the National Oceanic and Atmospheric Administration. Suzanne had walked the decks of the *Porpoise IV* from day one, traveling all along the eastern and western seaboards of America, searching for clues for the cause in rising global temperatures and their impact on the biosphere. It could host a crew of fifteen, most of them climate scientists, with a max out of forty days at sea.

The *Porpoise IV* was more her home than her condo back in Redondo Beach.

Right now, they were forty miles off the coast of Cuba, studying the latest pocket of methane gas being released from the deep ocean floor. Methane levels had been rising all around the globe, with the potential to eclipse any man-made pollutants to the atmosphere. If ocean water temperatures rose enough to thaw the tremendous stores of frozen methane gas, they could kiss the ozone, and mankind, goodbye.

"Holding steady from yesterday," Tom Mitchelson said, staring at the bank of computer screens. "Not enough to worry ourselves about."

She gave the NOAA climatologist a playful punch on the arm. "Oh sure, for the short term."

He shrugged, eyes glued to the data pouring in. "I like to live in the now."

"Could it harm any refugees trying to get to the Florida coast?"

"Nah, anyone swimming or boating through that will be fine. They may get nauseous from the smell, but it won't kill them."

Suzanne plopped into the chair next to him. "Thank goodness for small favors." She ran her fingers through her long red hair made knotty by the salty air. Plopping her feet on the edge of the table, she checked out the tan on her long legs that went so far as the bottom cuff of her shorts. She was out on the water and in the sun all the time, but almost never in a bathing suit. She made a note to double up on the moisturizer. Her skin was getting flaky. "With the way the Gulf Stream has been changing, we might find ourselves stuck here for a long while. And this," she tapped at the monitor feeding video of the bubbling water, "is just the tip of the iceberg."

Tom handed her a manila folder. "Or, maybe not."

"What's this?"

"Coast Guard sent it over about ten minutes ago."

Suzanne opened the folder and read the printed emails. She reached for her cigarettes, remembering that she'd quit yet again five days ago.

"That's awful close to the coast," she said, tugging at her bottom lip.

"Close enough to check out the sights on South Beach," Tom said, grinning despite the severity of the news.

"Not funny, Tom," she muttered, pacing with her eyes glued to the pages.

Leaning back in his seat, Tom replied, "Well, it's kinda funny."

"This is some serious shit. And it just popped up today?"

"At least it was discovered today."

Suzanne pulled and pulled at her lip until she tasted copper. She said, "I need Marlboros. Better get us to Miami."

FIVE

He was actually doing it!

Years of studying Hemingway in college, then getting his Masters in American Literature, followed by trips to Paris, Idaho and Illinois, Bob Hanover was one step further in his quest to walk in Papa's shoes.

Marlin fishing off Key West.

He was tempted to pinch himself, but the sunburn he'd gotten the day before when he'd passed out on the beach after downing one too many frozen daiquiris discouraged him from doing so.

"You want more water?" his buddy and traveling companion, Ryan Morrow, said. Ryan wore a huge straw hat, the kind old ladies donned to stay out of the sun. It even had three straw flowers on the front, painted blue, pink and yellow.

"I'm good," Bob said. "And please take that stupid hat off."

"Not a chance, bud. Unlike you, I have very little turf up top and my scalp is screaming today. I'm not adding to the pain. Here, drink it," he said, handing him an ice-cold bottle of water. "You gotta rehydrate. If you snag a marlin, you'll need your strength."

"Fine," Bob said. He chugged the entire bottle without coming up for air. Jesus, he was thirstier than he thought. Turning to the captain of the private boat that he'd rented for no small sum, he shouted through the wind, "How much further?"

The captain, a burly Cuban with what looked to be a permanent five o'clock shadow, said, "I'm actually about to stop now."

There was one other person aboard, a young guy who went by the name Stick. Bob assumed Stick wasn't his government name, but rather a reference to his long, lean body. Stick was there to assist should he catch a marlin. In fact, if he did, it was going to be all hands on deck. The big fish were fearsome fighters. Bob had hit the gym hard the past three months, strengthening his arms and core. He was on hallowed ground out here, or water to be precise. He didn't want Hemingway looking down thinking he was a pussy.

When the engine cut off, the silence was overpowering. The waters were relatively calm. They were so far out, land was a distant memory. Even the seagulls were nowhere in sight.

Ryan clapped him on the back. "You ready, big guy?"

Bob winced. His friend's hand felt like needles jabbing his sunburn. No matter. He was jazzed and ready to do this. "Hell yeah."

Stick gathered the necessary supplies – a special rod made just for marlin fishing, fighting belt that would secure the rod to his waist, non-slip gloves, 8-foot fly gaff and a toolbox filled with cutters, pliers, hooks and more.

"You want to dip a line in, too?" Bob asked his friend.

"Nope. I'm just here to enjoy the open sea. In fact, I may take a nap. While you'll be exhausted when we get back, I'll be ready to hit the bars again. I cannot believe how hot the chicks are down here."

Bob chuckled, "It doesn't hurt that a lot of them just happen to lose their tops as the night wears on."

"That it doesn't."

"Okay, why don't you sit in that chair and I'll get you all set up," Stick said with just the slightest tinge of a French accent.

Bob's heart began to gallop. Fucking marlin fishing right where Hemingway snagged his own trophies. And with a mate from France. Maybe he even drank in some of the same Paris cafes that Hemingway frequented. "Make sure you start recording when I get one," he said to Ryan.

"I even brought a spare charger just in case, bro." Ryan lay on a cushioned bench, using the hat to cover his face and chest.

Settling into the hardback chair, Bob looked over the water. Below it, somewhere, was a worthy adversary. He recounted various Hemingway passages about the art of fishing the deep, the words a relaxing poetry to Bob's excitable brain.

"Dude, you think this constitutes stalking?" he said.

Ryan replied, "Nah, it's not stalking if the guy you're following is dead. Think of it more as attending Papa's Ultimate He-Man School."

They both laughed, with Stick and the captain looking at them as if they were complete morons.

Something thumped against the boat, rocking it and throwing Stick off balance.

"What the hell was that?" Ryan said, sitting up.

"Shark maybe?" Bob said.

The captain and Stick looked overboard on each side of the boat. Bob scanned the surface for a telltale dorsal fin, cursing all sharks everywhere. Damn scavengers. If they didn't clear the area of marlin, surely they would do their best to take their pound of flesh once he hooked one.

"What about one of those big sea turtles?" Ryan said.

"No, not a turtle," Stick said. He turned back to them, smiling. "It's okay. Just a little bump in the road."

Bob was about to joke with him that bad humor would affect his tip when two sharp concussions sent all of them on their asses.

Ryan's face, previously red as a fire hydrant, drained of all color. "Oh crap, oh crap, oh crap!" he shouted.

The captain scrabbled on his hands and knees, opening a console by the wheel. His hand came out gripping a formidable-looking handgun.

After that, no one dared move.

If we're being targeted by sharks, we're dead, Bob thought. *We're so far away from the coast! What else could knock a forty-foot boat like that?*

If they were lucky, it was a passing pod of whales.

Bob wasn't feeling very lucky at the moment.

"Why don't you get us out of here?" he said, glaring at the captain.

The dull haze of confusion in the captain's eyes dissolved. "Yes. Yes, I'll take us someplace else."

Ryan dared to lift himself up and peer over the side of the boat. "I don't see anything." He kept his eyes on the water, the wind blowing the ridiculous hat off his scarlet head.

The engine bellowed, the captain secure in his seat, one hand on the throttle, the other on the wheel.

Bob felt his spirits buoyed. Maybe it was a passing pod of whales and they could salvage the day, just drop the line a little closer to civilization than they'd originally planned.

But the captain and Stick looked utterly bugged out. What the hell could scare them like that?

The boat made a forty-five degree turn, churning foam and heading to safety. Bob's breath returned to him, and he greedily gobbled as much air as his lungs could handle. For a second, Bob had to grab hold of his chair as the boat slid hard to the right.

"Now I need a beer," he said. "Ryan, you want one, too?"

He turned to his friend and screamed.

The remains of his flattened head lay on the deck, spewing blood and brain matter. His legs and arms twitched. It looked as if someone had placed his skull in a giant vise and cranked it as far as it could go.

"Holy shit!" Stick yelled behind him.

Bob didn't have time to scramble to Ryan's side as the boat slammed into something large enough to send it airborne, tilting on its side a moment before crashing back into the ocean. Ryan's jittering body slipped out of sight. Bob dove with every ounce of strength in his rubbery legs, desperate to clear himself from the flipped boat.

In an instant, the boat was a wreck, the captain and Stick nowhere to be seen. Bob kicked harder than he should, flapping his arms to stay afloat. If he kept this pace up, he'd be exhausted and drowning in minutes. His eyes stung with tears.

"Ryan!"

He knew Ryan couldn't hear him. Ryan was dead. His brain was all over the place, for Christ's sake! What could have done that to him? What fish had the stealth to kill a man without anyone noticing?

No longer caring what Hemingway's ghost thought of him, Bob wept, clinging to the exposed and dented hull of the boat.

A lifejacket. He needed a lifejacket. Didn't the better ones have some kind of beacon? Or was that just in movies?

He didn't see any floating around. That's because they were stowed in a storage container in the stern. He could swim under and find it, until the air trapped underneath seeped away and the boat sank for good.

"Stick? Captain?"

No reply.

There was zero chance for survival without a lifejacket. Back in high school, he'd failed to make the swim team and couldn't pass the simple lifeguard test for two straight summers.

Taking a deep, ragged breath, Bob slipped under the boat.

When he opened his eyes, several pairs of black orbs stared back at him.

The air exploded from his lungs.

What the hell were those things?

They weren't sharks and they sure as hell weren't whales. They looked like something straight from a drive-in horror movie.

And they were huge!

Despite his terror, he glanced back just before breaking the surface. Their gaping maws were wide open, but they didn't have any teeth.

When the first one clamped down on his leg, he felt the muscle and meat explode from his skin like an overfilled sausage casing. The pain was beyond comprehension. He opened his mouth to scream, taking on a dangerous lungful of water.

His other leg simply popped as another creature grabbed hold.

Bob's luck wasn't all bad.

He passed out a second before a third chomped on his torso. He never felt his heart rocket up his neck, lodging in the back of his throat.

SIX

Whit walked out of the hospital in a daze. Nestor Garza was waiting for him by the turnabout, engine running, chill from the air conditioner knifing his bones when he opened the door.

"How is he?" Nestor asked. "I saw his picture on the news. He looks a little like a young Matthew McConaughey."

Slumping in the chair, wishing he had an extra large Bloody Mary in his hands right about now, Whit exhaled heavily. "He's dead."

Nestor slapped the steering wheel. "What? That's a shame. Such a young kid. They said he was bad, very bad. Was it an infection from the amputation? I've read that that happens more than people think, especially with all those wounded soldiers coming in from the Middle East."

"They didn't tell me. No reason to share that kind of information with an ichthyologist who shows up out of nowhere. I wish I knew someone around here I could get to pull some strings. That's the problem with being overseas for five years. I'm completely out of the loop. If this was Australia, I'd be set. I have to get my hands on his blood work and find out what kind of toxin that fish pumped into his system."

Pulling away from the hospital, Nestor said, "Call Julie May."

The car immediately said it was dialing.

"Who's Julie May?" Whit asked, anxious to get back to the chimaera.

"A friend who knows everyone. If you need someone to get you access to that boy's information, she's the one to go to."

Whit smiled at the man. "Nestor, you're turning out to be handier than Tabasco sauce at an oyster eating contest."

By the time they got back to the Seaquarium, Julie May, who sounded like the embodiment of positivity and light, assured them she'd get Whit all the access he needed before the end of the day. Whit was impressed.

"What does Julie do?" he asked as they got out of the car. He was grateful to be out of the ice box of a car.

"She's done just about everything. Started as a model, married young and rich, opened a couple of clubs, restaurants, dated the governor after she caught her first husband cheating on her. A lot of people owe her favors, and the ones that don't just love her."

"And you know her how?"

"We were each other's first loves in grammar school. I remind her all the time I was the one who got away," he said with a childlike grin.

Whit was starting to like Nestor more and more. "Come on, let's find out how a fish that shouldn't be managed to kill a full-grown man."

Dhalia Shields sat on a rolling chair by the tank containing the chimaera. She looked relieved to see them.

"I assume our boys from the University haven't shown up yet," Whit said, heading straight for the mysterious fish.

"They just called for directions. I figure they're about ten minutes away."

Whit shook his head. "How do you get lost when every phone has a GPS?"

"If they're with the marine biology department, you'd think they'd know where to find the sole aquarium in town."

"All work and no play," Whit said distractedly, his mind fully fixated on the chimaera fish.

You shouldn't even be here. No, you're Australian for ancient fish, not some retiree looking to spice things up in Miami. What the hell did you eat along the way to get this big? And were you alone?

He understood why people called the fish a ghost shark. It did resemble a shark with a long body, extrusive dorsal fin and large, emotionless eyes. And yes, it was a distant relative, but distant in the way of hundreds of millions of years of evolutionary paths winding away from one another. Most grew to two, maybe three feet. This one here, it was something else.

Whit had seen his share of chimaera fish in the waters between Australia and New Zealand, their primary habitat, though they'd been spotted in the southern parts of Africa. They were deep-sea fish, observed mostly in submersibles or underwater cameras. As deadly as they appeared, they actually didn't have teeth like a shark. Instead, their cartilaginous tooth plates were used to crush shellfish, not tear and grind them apart.

What concerned him most was its length and why it was so off course. Even at this size, it should not have been able to produce enough toxin to take a man's life. He was beginning to wonder if he was dealing with some kind of mutation or hybrid, despite all appearances confirming it as 100% chimaera. He'd find out more when he had a chance to dissect it.

Dhalia's phone chirped, breaking him from quiet deliberation.

"They're here," she said, the heels of her shoes clacking on the marble floor as she left to let the University crew in.

Whit patted the side of the fish. "We're going to get real intimate."

Nestor spoke up. "Be careful. You're dealing with a murderer."

A chill danced up Whit's spine. He pulled his hands from the water.

SEVEN

The *Porpoise IV* was on course for Miami under a clear night sky. Suzanne Merriweather bummed a smoke from Shirley Palmer, one of the scientists aboard with an affinity for doing and saying anything that was against the current climate of political correctness.

"I never even considered smoking until they started banning it everywhere," she'd said, handing over a couple of Kool menthols. "This country is fucked. Pretty soon they're going to tell us sex is bad for us and we'll be forced to donate eggs and sperm to government controlled fertilization centers where they can genetically manipulate everything to wipe out what they consider weak traits."

Suzanne mussed Shirley's green Mohawk. The woman was her age, a shade over thirty, a little on the old side for those kinds of fashion statements, but on her, it worked.

"Didn't they do that in that movie *Logan's Run*?" Suzanne asked, dropping the cigarettes in her shirt pocket.

"The sci-fi writers know their shit. They can see beyond the tips of their noses while the powers that be anesthetize the masses."

"You do realize you work for the government, right?"

Shirley smirked. "Safest place to be is on the inside, Suzie."

She patted her shoulder. "Just be sure to warn me before you decide to take it all down."

"I have my lists. Don't worry, you're on the good one."

Shirley put her noise-canceling headphones back on, most likely listening to Rage Against the Machine or Fugazi. She was quirky, and that was putting things mildly, but she was also damn good at her job.

She was just as concerned by the methane readouts outside Miami as Suzanne. If what the Coast Guard had reported was right, that was one mammoth vent, but not enough to bring down a ship or passing plane. It sounded silly, but recent theorists had speculated that massive methane expulsions were responsible for many of the disappearances in the Bermuda Triangle. This particular methane release was right on the lower left third of the infamous triangle.

Oh God, please don't let the nuts get wind of this, Suzanne thought, admiring the panoply of stars above her.

The reality was, underwater landslides could sometimes free up frozen pockets of prehistoric methane gas. The bubbles rise up from the sea floor, expanding in size as they ascend. When they reach the surface, they burst, releasing their gaseous contents.

The crackpot theory du jour was that massive methane bubbles or a high concentration of hundreds or thousands of them bursting underneath a boat would draw it right into the ocean, the hollowness of the bubbles acting like a gigantic suction device. Kind of like a Bermuda Hoover. There were quite a few believers in this theory, mostly because it didn't involve alien abduction or space wormholes. It sounded plausible enough for the uninformed.

What people didn't realize was that the decreasing incidences of planes and ships disappearing in the Triangle just happened to coincide with leaps in navigation and weather predicting technology. Climatologists like Suzanne had a hand in that, but it wasn't sexy enough to sell on a cable special about the mysteries of the sea. So much for common sense.

She let the smoke linger in her lungs longer than she should have, savoring the warm feeling it gave off. Sputtering as she exhaled, Suzanne tried to clear her mind. It was best to get some rest now. Tomorrow was a new, busy day.

Letting the wind caress her face, eyes closed, she didn't hear Tom Mitchelson's frantic footsteps come up behind her. When he touched her shoulder, she yelped, dropping her cigarette into the churning ocean.

"Sorry," he said. "We just heard a distress call, not far from here. Sounds like a commercial fishing boat is having some serious trouble. We're closer than the nearest Coast Guard ship and heading over to see what we can do to help."

Suzanne went rigid. Out on the ocean, even the simplest problem could escalate to a matter of life and death in seconds.

"Did they say what was wrong?"

"I'm...I'm not sure. All I heard is that someone might be dead and they're thinking of abandoning ship."

Feeling the muscles in her stomach coil, Suzanne followed him inside. A night of relaxation just wasn't in the cards.

Antonio Maia stared in mute horror at the pancaked remains of Devon McDonald. His shipmate of the past month slid from side to side on the deck as the ship swayed, blood and entrails leaking from horrid splits in his body.

The creature that had done it to him was dead, a gaffer's pole embedded in its eye.

It was a fish the likes of which none of them had ever seen.

And it wasn't alone.

"Hook it, dammit, hook it!" Lou Argenon shouted. Each man gripped long silver hooks used to haul in nets. Right now, the sharp hooks were their only defense against the horde of demon fish that had spilled from their overflowing trawling nets.

Antonio lunged at the ten-foot fish about to clamp its mouth on Lou's leg. Just missing being impaled by its dorsal fin, he straddled the massive, plated head, burying the hook as deep as it could go. Ice cold brains oozed over his hand.

The fish slipped away from him as the boat listed. Lou turned to Antonio, his face pale as death.

"We have to get the hell off the deck," he said, chest heaving, covered from head to toe in blood.

"I know, but how?" Antonio said.

Of the ten strange fish that had poured from the first net, four were bunched up by the door leading to the galley. Their great mouths worked in heaving gasps. If there were no other live, ravenous fish on the deck, he and Lou could wait until the big beasts died.

Unfortunately, they had four other live monsters to contend with. Not to mention however many were in the other net that hovered overhead. The mast and winch groaned under the weight. Pretty soon, they would give way and a fresh load of death would come spilling atop them.

"We could try going over and using the guard railing to work our way around them to the wheelhouse," Lou said.

"There's no way we'd make it. One slip up and we're in the drink." When Lou failed to grasp the full extent of what he meant, he added, "Right where those things are!"

Lou shook him off. "We've been bottom trawling. I bet they're probably not near the surface."

"I don't like that word, *probably*."

"It's better than *definitely* getting squashed if we stay here."

They looked to Devon, his body tangled up with the remains of their extra net. When that fish had dropped from the net, grabbing onto him like a steel trap sent by a vengeful God, they didn't have time to help him. The creature compressed his body as easily as stepping on a marshmallow.

"Look out!" Antonio shouted.

One of the fish, at least a twelve-footer, squirmed its hefty body toward them, its mouth open wide. They jumped to their right, Lou ending up in front of another fish. It slammed its jaws down on his ankle, crushing the bone to powder, muscles to mush. His scream of agony nearly shattered Antonio's eardrum.

"Get it off me! Get it off me!" he wailed as the fish released its grip for a fraction of a second, just enough to claim more of his leg.

Antonio had landed in the messy remains of Devon, slipping and falling on his back. His friend's gore washed over him, some of it getting in his mouth. Woozy from fear and revulsion, he scrambled to his feet just as a wave sent him off balance again.

Something punctured his back. His hand went right to the spot, squeezing hard. It felt as if someone had injected acid into his lower back. A giant fish slid away from him.

What did it stab me with?

"Help me, Antonio," Lou pleaded. The fish now had him up to his knee. His blood poured from the fish's mouth.

The pain left Antonio breathless. Turning around, he skipped away just before one of the creatures could get ahold of him. He noticed the spiny protrusions at the front of its head. He must have landed on one of them.

"What did you put in me?" he cursed the fish. He could feel his kidney liquefying, piss bursting from it like a ruptured plastic bag, flooding his body with toxins. "You son of a bitch!" He spit on the fish. It stared back at him, devoid of emotion, the look of an apathetic Grim Reaper.

"Please, please, Antonio, you have to pull me out!"

Antonio collapsed, the fire now in his lungs, his heart, his brain. He couldn't help Lou, just as his shipmate couldn't help him. Deckhands on a fishing boat were always expendable.

EIGHT

Whit stepped into the harsh light of a chilly morning – chilly for Miami, which meant temps in the low sixties. The sun made his eyes water and he had to use his hands to shield them as he stumbled down the steps.

The fluorescent lighting in the lab at Florida International University wore on him after a while. He'd been out in the field so long, he wasn't used to being pent up indoors for long stretches of time.

He checked his watch.

8:35AM.

He'd been working on the chimaera fish for over twelve hours. The student assistants the dean had been nice enough to volunteer had clocked out hours ago. He saw they were exhausted despite their growing fascination at the unique specimen before them.

Of course, they hadn't spent their lives studying the chimaera, so it didn't have the same magnetic pull as it did for Whit. All along, he kept expecting to find something in its biology that would prove him wrong, that it wasn't in fact a chimaera, but perhaps an as yet undiscovered offshoot of the family tree.

Those thoughts had been dashed about six hours ago, but there was still plenty of testing on blood and tissue that needed to be done.

No, this was just one big fucking chimaera.

Big and lost, he thought.

Samples of the toxin extracted from the chimaera fish were to be sent to one of his colleagues in San Diego. He'd roomed with Garrett Harmon, now Dr. Harmon, when they were undergrads at the University of San Diego. His old friend fell in love with the city, opting for a career in lab work so he could stay there. Whit felt bad calling him in the middle of the night, but Garrett seemed excited at the chance to find out what kind of noxious stew had been percolating in the chimaera. As far as Whit was concerned, there was no one better to call on for the job.

It was a Saturday, so the campus was empty, especially at this hour. He expected to see one or two students making the walk of shame. The quadrangle was devoid of life, aside from some chirping birds that sounded like the bells of Notre Dame to his tired brain.

I need a drink.

Coffee was not his craving at the moment. The taxi arrived five minutes after his call.

"Where to?" the cabbie asked. He was older, possibly in his late sixties, with a full, gray beard, bushy salt and pepper eyebrows and skin as tan as a leather belt.

"Any liquor stores open nearby?" Whit said, sinking into the seat.

"I know a couple less than a mile from here."

"You pick."

The cab swerved through a roundabout, Whit closing his eyes. There was no way he was going to get any sleep if he didn't shut his mind down for a while.

They stopped in front of a place called Sal's Liquor Emporium, though it's narrow aisles and meager wares didn't exactly scream *emporium*. Whit found a bottle of Michael Collins whiskey, paid for it in cash, and was sipping from it before he got back in the cab.

"Rough night?" the swarthy cabbie asked.

"Just trying to avoid a rough day. You can drop me off at the Hyatt on Biscayne Boulevard." He rolled down his window, greedily sucking in the morning air between hits of Michael Collins. The Irish whiskey burned his throat, in a good way. He figured if he timed it right, he'd be ready to pass out by the time he got to his room. The drink also steadied the tremor in his hands.

To his credit, the cabbie wasn't a talker. Whit wasn't sure how well he'd hold up under casual conversation at the moment. Of course, the man probably thought he was a drunk and it was best to leave him to himself. He couldn't blame him. He'd think the same if their roles were reversed.

Driving down Route 1, he could smell the ocean. He wondered if there were more chimaeras like the one back at the University, bottom feeding in the dark, keeping close to the coast since it was mating season.

"It's mating season down under, not here," he said, his gaze catching glimpses of stores and cars and people as they sped past.

"What's that?" the cabbie said.

Yep, he definitely thinks I'm some rummy.

"Nothing. Just thinking out loud. I'm an ichthyologist. The kind of fish I study are entering their mating season now."

There, that should clear things up. I'm not your everyday drunk. I have a title I'm sure you've never heard of and I study fish when they fuck.

Whit chortled, nearly spitting up a mouthful of whiskey.

Why did he feel he needed to justify himself to a guy he'd never see again?

The cab eased under the carport in front of the Hyatt. Whit checked the meter, saw he owed fifteen bucks. Not bad. He wondered how much more it would have cost had it been later in the day with traffic.

"All you," he said, handing the cabbie twenty-five bucks.

"Thank you," he replied, stuffing the cash in his shirt pocket.

And now you're overcompensating, Whit thought.

Somehow managing to jam the bottle in the thigh pocket of his cargo shorts, Whit rode the elevator to the tenth floor, got the key card to work after six swipes, turned the air conditioner off, opened a window the small crack that was allowed and sat on the edge of the bed. He took one last pull from the bottle, saw it was halfway gone, and lay down.

The sound of kids laughing in the room next to him bled through the thin walls.

Closing his eyes, he saw the chimaera, not on the dissection table, but in its habitat. The oily looking fish skulked along the ocean floor, gobbling up anything in its path, growing bigger by the second. A yellowish substance leaked from a sharp tendril atop its head.

Poison.

So much poison, it couldn't contain it within its own massive body.

The chimaera saw him, changed its lazy course, heading now in his direction.

Whit was frozen, his feet welded to the ocean floor. He could breathe under water, but he was too terrified to move a muscle, much less draw a breath.

It raced toward him, wide mouth open, hunger in its cold, alien eyes.

The *Porpoise IV* had come upon true horror last night. The smell of vomit was overwhelming on board. Suzanne had lost half her stomach when she saw the remains of the men on the fishing trawler. She wasn't alone. For most of the crew, it was the first time they'd seen a dead body outside a wake.

The lone survivor of the fishing trawler was the captain, a man named Moe Holiday, who had locked himself in the wheelhouse after watching his entire crew get wiped out by the enormous, bizarre fish they had snagged in their nets.

By the time the *Porpoise IV* had arrived, the damage had been done. Both men and fish were dead. A bulging net was held aloft, weighted down by a catch of quickly rotting fish that defied classification.

They'd managed to get Holiday out of the wheelhouse and onto the Porpoise *IV*. Shirley Palmer slipped him a Valium from her private stash, along with some herbal tea. He took it without asking what it was, downing the tea and staring into space.

The Coast Guard arrived within the hour. The trawler was awash with harsh lights from the Guard cutter and the *Porpoise IV*, the carnage on the deck in stark, naked relief. The blood looked redder than it should, the pulp of the men's interior organs, savaged and squeezed through orifices and burst flesh, a miasma of gray and pink and purple.

It was beyond awful.

"I feel like we should surround the ship in crime scene tape," Tom Mitchelson said, sipping on a cup of coffee. They watched the Coast Guard do their thing, their stomachs obviously much stronger than those on the scientific vessel.

"Right now, it is a crime scene," Suzanne said.

Two Guardsmen were talking to the captain now, though they weren't getting too far. The man was down to one syllable answers, either in shock or clamming up until he had a lawyer present.

"You think that guy did all that?" Tom asked.

Suzanne couldn't take her eyes off the dead fish. Something about them was familiar. She just couldn't put her finger on it.

"I think humans are capable of anything," she said.

"But how could he squash a guy like that?"

They looked at the body of the man who appeared to have been put in a machine press.

Flat Stanley, Suzanne thought. The moment the character from the children's book flashed into her mind, she wanted to kick herself for making light of it.

But that's exactly what he reminded her of – a grisly Flat Stanley.

"There are lots of heavy things on that ship. Holiday could have dropped it on him."

"And those other two?"

That was harder to explain. They looked diseased, their flesh mottled in bruises, swollen as if they'd been in the water for a couple of days, mouths, eyes and ears leaking vital fluids turned a leprous yellow.

She sighed, the acid of her vomit still burning her throat. "I have no frigging idea. Just like I haven't a clue what they caught in those nets. You ever see anything like it?"

Shaking his head, Tom said, "I spend my time looking at computer monitors or to the sky. What's under the sea is a mystery to me. At first, I thought they were sharks, but I was clearly wrong. I've never seen a shark that color and looking like that."

The big fish were marbled brown and gray, with thick bodies and snub noses. She couldn't make out if they had sharp rows of teeth, or any teeth for that matter.

The rest of the *Porpoise IV* crew and scientists had gone back to their bunks, overwhelmed from the excitement. Storms they could handle. The wreck of human carnage was not in their purview.

"You're right, they do look like sharks," Suzanne said, squinting to get a better look at the fish with the pole sticking out from its head. At least it hadn't been a one-sided slaughter. There were no winners on either side. The fish the men didn't kill had died from suffocation.

Something was falling into place.

"Sharks," Suzanne repeated.

No, not sharks at all. But *like* sharks. They could be...

Not here. Not this big.

"I'll be right back," she said. She ran to her bunk, grabbing her phone and returning to the deck. She zoomed in as best as she could on the fish, taking great pains not to get any of the dead men in the frame. Snapping off a couple dozen pictures, most of them grainy because of distance and the bobbing motion of both ships, she went through each one, enlarging them as best she could on her phone's palm-sized screen.

God, they were hideous.

"I think I know what these things might be related to, at the very least," she said with Tom peering over her shoulder. She could smell his coffee breath before the briny air overpowered it.

"What do you think they are?" he asked.

Her stomach, already a ball of tension, tightened some more.

"I'm not entirely sure, but someone I was once related to might know."

NINE

Cursing, Whit lashed out, sweeping his phone, alarm clock and bottle of whiskey off the bedside table.

His phone kept chiming away, signaling to him that messages were coming through. He thought he'd set the damn thing to mute so he could get some uninterrupted sleep.

Head inching over the side of the bed, he looked down at the glowing red numerals on the alarm clock.

11:17AM.

Just over two hours sleep was not enough. Not even close.

There was a brief temptation to check his phone so he knew who to put a hex on later for waking him up. The sight of the whiskey, the cap having fallen off, the contents glugging onto the carpet, made his head hurt. The Michael Collins cost fifty bucks. That was about twenty-five seeping into the garish rug.

"What a waste."

His head throbbed and his eyes felt as if they'd been drained of every last ounce of ocular fluid. Blinking was akin to poking needles in his skull.

When he closed them next, he made sure they stayed closed. Working hard to fall back to sleep, his phone beeped and sang away, oblivious to the pain and suffering of its master.

An expert at being able to catch as many Zs as possible whenever the opportunity presented itself, Whit eventually fell back to sleep. This time, there were no chimaera nightmares.

The knocking on his door was much harder to ignore.

One eye popped open. Whit waited for a female voice to announce, "Room service."

Not this time. Three more raps on the door.

He waited.

Now four more knocks, harder this time.

"Who is it?" he croaked.

The reply was muffled by the door.

"Who?"

"Nestor."

"Shit balls." Whit sat up in bed, tugging at his hair. His head felt better. The clock on the floor showed him it was midafternoon. "Hold on, Nestor, I'm coming."

Whit was still in the clothes he'd worn yesterday. He was sure he smelled of chemicals, fish and booze. Nestor might regret this visit.

Opening the door, he was greeted by the Hispanic man's wide smile. He was holding a tan envelope in one hand, a cup of coffee in the other.

"I heard you had a late night," Nestor said.

Whit ushered him in, clinging to the doorknob for a moment to steady himself. "Or an early morning, depending on your point of view. For me?" he asked, eyeing the coffee.

"Thought you might need it."

Whit pulled back the plastic lid, tossing it on top of the dresser. Splotches of coffee sprinkled on the faux mahogany. It was hot and bitter. Just what he needed. Ambling to the chair by the window, he sat down, pulling the blinds aside. The sky was an unbroken blue, a plane sailing off in the distance.

"Have a seat, Nestor. You're making me nervous."

"I have a present for you," Nestor said, dropping the envelope on the small round table between the two chairs. "Early toxicology reports on the mate that died from that fish's sting. I can't remember the name. It's a chi...chi"

"Chimaera. According to Webster's, the word is based on a creature of mythology, an amalgam of different species in one terrifying beast. Or, in the current vernacular, one ugly fucker."

Nestor gave a short chuckle. "That's a perfect definition of your fish."

Whit picked up the envelope. "Not my fish. That guy belongs to Mother Nature. I'm just the man who spends an inordinate amount of time around them. Now, let's see what we have here."

Scanning two pages, the word *inconclusive* was used quite a lot. That was usually the problem with early lab results.

"Any chance your old girlfriend could get a copy of the final report when it's ready?"

"No problem. She already told me she has someone on the lookout for us. It may be a few more days."

A few more days.

Would he still be here, or back in Australia by then?

He'd done all he could here. Out of professional curiosity, he needed to know what had killed the mate. Perhaps it was an allergic reaction to the toxin, a poison innocuous to all except this unfortunate guy who was in the wrong place at the wrong time. It could even be a chemical reaction between the chimaera toxin and something else that was in his blood. Maybe he was on medication, prescription or recreational.

Noticing Nestor's gaze locked on the scattered contents of the night table, Whit said, "Must have wigged out in my sleep." He gave a half smile he figured looked grotesque on his haggard face.

"I wouldn't light a match in here if I was you," Nestor said.

The sweet smell of the Michael Collins made Whit both nauseous and thirsty.

"I think I'll have to leave the maid a bigger tip," Whit said, shuffling the papers back into the envelope. He pushed it toward Nestor.

"No, those are yours to keep," he said.

"Thank you. I hope they didn't send you to drive me around today. There's really not much for me to do. I was thinking of grabbing a late lunch and maybe walking the beach."

And checking international flights.

"No, I just wanted to stop by and give you this. And also to thank you for letting me see the fish, even though I had a nightmare about it last night. I don't think I'll ever forget it. Here's my card. If you ever need anything, just let me know. Yesterday was fun."

Whit laughed, pulling the flesh of his face back with his calloused hands. "Yeah, it was fun all right. I think I have more questions than answers."

"Let's hope that was the first and last of them."

Nestor left, making sure to close the door behind him quietly. After peeing and drinking two glasses of water from the bathroom tap, Whit plucked the empty whiskey bottle, dumping it in the small trashcan. He put the alarm clock back on the table, grateful he hadn't broken it.

His phone was last. It showed he had fifteen text messages waiting for him.

Texting had never been his thing, nor were emails. He realized they were a necessary evil, but he preferred the freedom of being disconnected. The only tether he required was his scuba gear when he was underwater, the place he felt most at home.

The first two messages were from his sister, Carolyn. His stomach dropped. She never texted.

His first thoughts were – *Mom or Dad just died. What if it was both?*

Thumb shaky from nerves, he opened the messages.

Hey Brad, gonna apologize right off the bat. Mom and Dad are fine.

She always could read his mind.

Got a frantic call from the love of your life. She seemed real determined to talk to you. Said there were pictures she had to send. I gave her your number because she sounded desperate. Please don't hate me. I'll pay for a new number of you want. – Luv you.

If there was one thing he couldn't do, it was hate his sister. Even though she and his ex had been close friends since childhood, Carolyn had taken his side in the divorce. Blood, sometimes, is thicker than water.

Taking a deep breath, he saw thirteen messages from Suzanne.

"Do I even look?" he said. There was no alimony, so she couldn't be after him for money. Maybe she'd gotten hitched, and wanted to rub her wedding pics in his face. He wasn't sure how he'd feel about that. Things had ended on a bitter note, but he wasn't sure he was ready to see her happy with another man just yet.

He opened her text string.

I know u don't want me to have your number, but this is important. I'm off the coast of Florida now. Came across something unreal last night. Coast Guard is here. Men on fishing trawler are dead.

Whit sat back in the chair. This is not what he was expecting.

The captain said his men were killed by huge fish they caught. I can't describe how horrible it is. U need to see these fish. Sending u pics. Call me if they are what I think they are. Are u still in Australia?

No, he was certainly not in Australia. For the first time since the divorce, he and Suzanne were sharing a time zone.

He opened the first picture and felt all the air escape his lungs.

More chimaera fish. Only these looked huge, even bigger than the one back at the University.

And they'd killed men.

How many? And how were they killed? Were the men stung, like the mate on the party boat?

Scrolling through the pictures, he saw giant chimaera killed on the deck, others suspended in a net. These things were the size of Great Whites, if his estimations were correct.

That can't be.

The one he saw was a baby compared to these.

Pacing around the room, he gave each picture a second look. The hairs on his arms stood on end. A sharp pain in his gut sent him running for the bathroom. He dry heaved until his ribs hurt.

Next, he did something he swore he'd never do.

He called his ex-wife.

TEN

Despite the excitement of the night before, there was still work to be done. Everyone aboard the *Porpoise IV* was bleary-eyed, moving a fraction faster than slow motion. The sharp aroma of coffee was everywhere.

"We're just about on top of it," announced Ken Beekman, the ship's captain, cutting the engine.

Suzanne spotted the bubbling water ahead of them, tapping Ken's shoulder. "Pay dirt," she muttered, chewing on a nail.

"You get paid for this?" Ken joked.

Raymond Basu, wearing a mask, lowered instruments into the water after taking readings of the air. He looked back at them and gave a thumbs-up. Suzanne was grateful he made the trip. As a climatologist, he was brilliant. With a scaled-down crew, she really needed his expertise. He was also great to have on board, always quick with a smile or joke, traits that came in handy when you were out at sea for long stretches.

Dark clouds were on the distant horizon. According to NOAA, the storm was heading further out to sea. Nothing for them to worry about.

"Okay, what do we have?" she asked Tom, who was busy opening up various windows on his monitors, each one reflecting various readings from the equipment Raymond had deployed.

"Christ, that's a lot," he said. His sandy hair was matted to one side and he needed a shave.

"Are we talking threat levels?"

He paused, eyes bouncing from one rising graph to the next. "No, but pretty close."

A rotten egg stench wafted through the room, overpowering the far more pleasing bouquet of coffee. Suzanne had long ago lost her olfactory revulsion. Was it normal to become acclimated to the rot of methane gas?

Shirley Palmer, dressed in a White Zombie T-shirt, black rubber bands on her wrists that went to her mid-forearms, waved at the air.

"Smells like my dogs after I feed them tripe," she said. "It may be healthy for them, but man, it sure doesn't feel good for me when they've digested it."

"Maybe we should pull back a little bit," Suzanne advised Ken. He nodded, goosing the engine. The sensors they'd lowered into the water were smack in the middle of the release vent.

"How far are we from the coast?" she asked Shirley.

"About fifty miles."

Suzanne rose from her seat to step outside and had to grip the back of the chair. She was dizzy and tired and still upset about what she saw last night. Plus, she hadn't heard back from Whit, which only added to her anxiety. Throw in the biggest release of methane she'd seen in the Atlantic, and it was no wonder her head was spinning.

Whit.

Even when her own last name was Whitley for those five tumultuous years, he'd insisted she call him Whit. He hated the name Brad. He'd said it made him sound like a trust fund baby.

He needn't have worried. He acted more like a beach bum than an aristocrat.

I wonder if he's even looked at what I sent. Knowing him, he probably deleted them, sight unseen. It was nice to talk to Carolyn again, though.

She hadn't realized how much she missed her friend until she heard her voice. She just wished it had been under better circumstances.

"We should send the submersible down," she said to Tom. "See what's cooking."

"Already on it."

Stepping outside didn't help her case of the spins. There was no fresh air to be found here, not until all of the gas had made its way to the surface and petered out.

Staring at the bubbling water, she thought of those old Godzilla movies, the ocean churning as he rose from the depths to either destroy or save Tokyo. As she got older, she realized the big old dinosaur always destroyed Tokyo, no matter his intentions. Construction companies would have made a killing rebuilding the city. As would the Mafia.

"This is what's going to wipe us out one day," Shirley said, startling Suzanne. "Forget factories and cars and cow farts."

"Ten years ago, I would have told you to stop talking like a conspiracy nut," Suzanne said. "But if this keeps stepping up all around the globe, it'll destroy the ozone within a hundred years."

They stood in silence, watching the crew prepare the submersible. It would send remote images and data to them, doing the dangerous work while they remained safe. They'd named it *Badass*. The little pink unmanned sub (they'd painted over the factory yellow) had done a lot of dirty work for them over the years, sometimes taking a beating in the process. But *Badass* kept on ticking.

Shirley said, "Well, we've had a good run. Kinda made a mess of things, but there've been plenty of good times."

With that, she left Suzanne's side.

We've had a good run. That's exactly what she'd said to Whit the day she asked for a divorce.

Whit used the hotel's printer so he could enlarge the images Suzanne had sent and actually handle them. He sat in a plush chair in the lobby, the pages spread over a table. He didn't even notice people stopping to take a peek as they walked by.

How the hell?

The phrase turned over in his mind again and again, like a leaf tumbling in the wind.

It stood to reason that where there was one, there would be others. Deep down, he'd hoped the chimaera he examined was a complete aberration, something that had gobbled up nuclear runoff.

Yeah, because 50's sci-fi movies were representations of pure science.

Chimaera fish had remained pretty much the same for hundreds of millions of years. They were not prone to sudden, or even gradual, mutations. They kept to themselves on the bottom of the sea where prying eyes were few and far between.

So then, *what the hell?*

He'd called Suzanne's phone and gotten her voicemail. Hearing her voice affected him more than he thought it would. An hour later, he still wasn't sure exactly how he felt – uneasy was maybe the best way to put it. It was like calling a girl for a first date, which was very strange.

Not as strange as those chimaera fish, which was why he had to talk to her.

"Chimaera fish the size of little yellow buses that kill people," he muttered. His stomach grumbled. Food was a rising priority.

"Eewwww, what are those?"

He looked up, meeting the repulsed stare of a little girl with the darkest eyes he'd ever seen, framed by curls of hair so blonde, it was almost white. She had to be six, seven tops.

Whit gathered the pictures into an askew pile.

"Are those fish or whales?" she asked.

Where are her parents? he thought. *Must be checking in.*

"I know that whales are mammals. They're not fish at all," she said, proud to show off her knowledge.

He grinned. "You're absolutely right. You're pretty smart."

"I love reading about the ocean. I saw a Beluga whale once at an aquarium."

Before he could stash the pages away, the girl plucked one from his hands. She studied it for a moment, her brows knit in intense concentration.

"They're gross."

He gingerly retrieved the printout. "They won't win any beauty contests, that's for sure. They're called chimaera fish and they live very deep in the ocean, far from here."

"That's a weird name."

"They're a weird fish."

"Are they in the aquarium?"

One was for a little while, he said to himself.

"In some aquariums, they do have small ones. They're very hard to find."

"Kathryn, leave the man in peace," a harried woman said, taking the girl by the hand. "I'm sorry if she disturbed you."

Whit shook his head. "Not at all. You have a budding marine biologist on your hands."

The woman shrugged her shoulders and mussed the girl's hair. "She's our little fish. We can't even plan a vacation unless there's an aquarium nearby. Kids find their paths. We parents are just along for the ride."

The girl waved to him as her mother led her to the elevators. Whit waved back.

Just along for the ride.

Walking to the hotel's dining room, Whit found Nestor's card in his pocket and made a call.

Flying back to Australia would have to wait.

ELEVEN

"Damn."

Suzanne saw that she'd missed Whit's call. Of course, he didn't leave a message. Why do that when he could keep her guessing what he thought of the pictures?

Maybe it was better that way. She felt like crap, and talking to Whit never made things better.

Well, not never, but most of the time, especially that last year.

"We have splashdown. *Badass* is going for a swim," Tom announced. "Cameras going live."

Three connected monitors blinked to life, showing nothing but rapidly rising bubbles. Durable little *Badass* just needed to take a short trip today – under fifteen hundred feet. In terms of ocean floor dives, this was akin to a trip to the corner store and back. The hope was to find the crack that was releasing the methane, measure it and make estimates as to how much of the gas was expected to rise before it sputtered out.

They would add that data to readings of the ozone, comparing it to historical findings which could give them an assessment of the impact rising methane levels had on modern and future climate.

Suzanne recalled how her research bored the hell out of her wild child of an ex. As if studying fish was as exciting as drag racing. He spent a lot of time in the water, sometimes facing danger, often exaggerating it to anyone who would listen at whatever bar he'd find himself in at the end of the day. He had a way of making his passion sound a hell of a lot cooler. It used to irritate her to no end. Now, years later, she couldn't latch on to just why that made her so upset.

As much as she wanted to call him again, there were more important things at hand. Holding her phone in her pocket, she leaned closer to the monitors.

"That's some major seltzer," Shirley said. Her Mohawk had gone limp, the green hairs flopping to one side.

"Badass is bumping along like a kite in a tropical storm," Tom said.

Two other men, Danny Garza and Simon DiNardo, were in charge of controlling *Badass*. They sat to Tom's right, headsets on, hands operating small joysticks, eyes glued to the camera feeds.

"It's like jumping into a mosh pit," Danny said. He was the youngest of the crew, looking like a fresh-faced teen when he was actually twenty-two. An avid gamer, he could operate remote vehicles better than most with tons of experience under their belts. Suzanne long suspected that Danny and Shirley shared more than a love for pop punk.

"You've spent plenty of time in those pits, so this should be a walk in the park," Simon deadpanned. He was twenty years Danny's senior, serious as a stroke, lightening up only when it was time to set *Badass* free. That was when he liked to rib his junior counterpart.

Suzanne checked outside to make sure the storm was still heading away from them. Yes, they had the best instruments in the world to predict storms, but Mother Nature had a habit of humbling the best of them.

Down the submersible went, the bigger bubbles near the surface giving way to smaller, clear orbs. Visibility was actually getting worse.

Simon started humming *Tiny Bubbles*. He did that every time they investigated methane releases. Danny groaned. "Please, not that again."

"Would you prefer I sing it?" Simon said.

"No," Suzanne interjected. It felt as if a nail were being driven into the center of her head. Simon's off-key baritone was the last thing she needed.

Tom looked up at her and shook his head. "You don't have to be here for this part. You look like crap on a cracker. Why don't you lie down for a bit?"

She waved him off. "I'll be fine. Plenty of time for sleep later."

"That's what we thought before that distress call."

"I'm betting lightning won't strike twice."

That brought a round of nervous laughter. You worked with NOAA long enough, you knew lightning struck twice more often than people suspected.

Suzanne blinked hard when the camera view shifted violently. They still saw only methane-filled bubbles, but it looked as if something had sideswiped *Badass.*

"What the hell was that?" she said.

Danny panned the unmanned sub's cameras around. Nothing out of the ordinary appeared.

"It wasn't a current," Simon said, his humming cut short.

The scene shifted again, the bow camera seeming to now point upward, fatter bubbles ascending ahead of it.

"Dolphin?" Shirley said. "Maybe it thinks it's a toy."

"I'll straighten *Badass* out and light the afterburners," Danny said.

Something large flashed by the starboard camera.

"Did you see that?" Suzanne said.

Tom's fingers flew over the keyboard. "I did and I'm pulling a still right now."

The blurry image of a long, wide body filled one of his monitors. It was hard to determine the color because it was obscured by the methane bubbles.

"I think we have our culprit," Tom said. "Whatever it is."

"I wish we could electrify *Badass,*" Danny said. "That would teach sea critters to mess with it. I don't want to have to spend the next week making repairs."

Shirley snorted. "This isn't a video game. You don't get points for frying everything in your way."

The rest of the descent went smoothly. It was darker than a tomb, but *Badass's* lights did their best to cut the terminal gloom.

"We getting close to the bottom?" Suzanne asked, chewing on what remained of the nail on her index finger. It was a nervous tic she'd thought she'd conquered.

That was before I spent the night looking at dead people and monster fish, she thought. She'd ask Shirley for another cigarette once *Badass* was back onboard.

"Just a couple hundred more feet," Simon replied, his allotment of merriment spent.

"Flip on the hull lights and camera," Suzanne said.

In just a minute, they'd see exactly what they were dealing with.

Down it went, time seeming to slow.

This was the part that always got to Suzanne, and the reason she didn't listen to Tom and take to her bunk. For all she knew, no one on earth had ever seen this portion of the ocean floor before. Each descent was a discovery.

"Holy jumping Jesus," Tom exclaimed.

Finally close enough to see the jagged crack in the sea floor, it stretched for as far as the powerful lights could reach.

But that was far from what made everyone hold their breath.

Methane wasn't the only thing pouring from the fissure.

Alien fish of remarkable size swarmed around the roiling vent. They broke free from the frozen depths, wriggling into the ocean. Some swam with astonishing speed in all directions, while others lingered about, as if they were waiting for others before venturing further into their new world.

"That can't be," Suzanne said. She had to grip the edge of Tom's desk to remain upright.

They were the very same fish that had killed those men on the trawler.

Except they looked even bigger.

"No freaking way," Shirley said. She sleepwalked to the monitors, eyes glazed over in wonderment. "It's like they're hatching from some kind of ancient incubator."

Simon yelled, "Danny, we have to pull up!"

Too late, they watched in horror as the giant fish took note of *Badass*. Mouths that looked big enough to crush a small car opened as they swam toward the sub. Simon and Danny never had a chance to save it. The pitch-black maws swallowed up the light, and everything died.

"They ate *Badass*," Danny said, slumped over the console. He looked as if he'd just lost a family member. Simon punched keys on the panel in front of him.

"All systems are down," he said. "She's gone."

Suzanne was so numb, she didn't even feel her teeth biting off a wedge of flesh on her fingertip. A sudden, stark realization set her heart into overdrive.

"We have to get the hell out of here, now!" she shouted.

Something told her if they didn't haul ass, the *Porpoise IV* and all her crew were next.

TWELVE

Thank God for Nestor and his connection, Julie May.

Whit, dressed in cargo shorts and an unbuttoned camp shirt adorned with pineapples and margarita glasses, jumped aboard the aluminum party boat. At a hundred feet long, it was a little more than he needed, but he wasn't about to gripe. The fact that he was borrowing it for free more than made up for that.

He turned to Nestor, who was holding his fedora onto his head. A sudden breeze whistled across the docks. "She's a beaut," he said. "Looks brand new."

"I think she is new," Nestor said. He didn't look too comfortable standing on the boat. The slightest sway had him grasping for something to hold on to. "Julie May said the fuel would be topped off and ready to go."

"But what about the guys who own it? They'll be out of the party fishing business as long as I'm tooling around on it."

"That's not a problem," a voice said behind them. A stocky man north of forty with straw hair bleached by the sun and skin bronzed like overcooked bacon stuck out his hand. "Travis Hewitt, welcome aboard." They shook, his grip like iron. "The *SenoRita* is my youngest child. Our mutual friend is compensating me for my time." He smiled, revealing teeth stained yellow.

"I can't thank you enough for lending your services," Whit said. "Nestor, you must have been one hell of a boyfriend to have Julie May footing the bill for this."

He gave them a sly smile. "I was quite the catch in my day. Besides, Julie is concerned about these fish. She's very protective of this city, and she doesn't want anything lurking around that can scare people off."

Travis chuckled. "When translated, that means loss of revenue. Sometimes you gotta spend money to save money."

Nestor's face darkened a bit, but Whit had to admit the grizzly seaman hit the nail right on the head. If people were afraid to fish the waters here, that meant less cash flowing through Julie May's properties. He made a note to ask Nestor just how much she owned.

"I guess it'll just be the two of us," Whit said.

"Three," Nestor said. "I'd like to stay, if that's okay with you."

The man already looked a lighter shade of green. Whit knew Nestor would regret his request within the hour, but he couldn't say no to the man. After all, without his help, he wouldn't be here right now.

"All right. You want to go grab some Dramamine from the store over there before we shove off?"

Shaking his head, Nestor said, "I'll be all right. I just need a little time to get my sea legs."

Travis said, "Actually, that now makes four. My son, Jim, is coming along, too. He's the *SenoRita's* first mate. Got him down below right now doing some last minute checks."

"Oh, I almost forgot," Whit said. He hopped back onto the dock, retrieving the scuba gear he'd borrowed from the University. His own gear was thousands of miles away. Travis helped him stow it away.

The younger Hewitt came up from below deck. He was very tall at six and a half feet with large, bony hands and an angular face. At first, Whit thought he was older, but once he saw his eyes, green as coral, he knew he was much younger, fresh out of college at most.

"You have the coordinates?" Whit asked the captain, the coordinates being the approximate spot where the first fishing boat had pulled the chimaera aboard.

"Already programmed," Travis said. He had a smile that seemed incomplete without the stub of a cigar sticking from the corner of his mouth. "In the immortal words of Burt Lancaster, 'Let's get wet!'"

Travis laughed like a maniacal Santa Claus, his son Jim rolling his eyes. "He's got a strange sense of humor, but he'll grow on you," he said, as if to apologize.

Whit had been around more men like Travis Hewitt than he could count. Something about the sun and salt water molded those crazy enough to spend their lives on the sea until they were a uniform lot.

"Some say I grow on people, but more like a fungus," Whit said.

The kid sputtered a small laugh and climbed up the small set of stairs to join his father in the pilothouse.

"You ready for what will most likely amount to an afternoon of complete boredom?" Whit asked Nestor.

The man took a seat, looking over the railing. Seagulls squawked nonstop, circling the *SenoRita*. He replied, "Isn't that the definition of fishing?"

Everyone was stunned.

Suzanne couldn't get the vision of the terrifying fish swarming *Badass* out of her head. The little submersible was gone. It would cost a fortune to replace. *Badass* had become their mascot over the years. It sounded silly, but losing it felt almost like losing a friend.

The crew was eerily quiet, even now that they were a good distance from the methane vent and the terrible creatures that sprang from it.

Every muscle and bone in her body was suddenly exhausted.

"What the hell was that?" she said to Tom.

"If we didn't have video proof, there's no way on God's green Earth I would tell the truth. The last thing I need is a psych evaluation and an order to keep my ass on land."

"Speaking of which, can you play it back?"

Bodies pressed together, huddled close to the monitor. Suzanne heard actual gasps when the first fish came into focus. Deep waters were home to some exceedingly unusual creatures, fish rarely seen in nature shows and never captured for an aquarium.

"Holy shit, look how many of them there are," Shirley whispered, her fingertips trembling over her glossy, bright pink lips.

Suzanne paused the video, the mass of fish frozen as they raced toward *Badass*.

"They look familiar to you all?" she said.

Tom sighed, pinching the bridge of his nose and crinkling his eyes.

"It's hard to tell for sure, but they look an awful lot like those fish on that trawler. Except bigger, if that's even possible."

"You think the Coast Guard was bright enough to keep one or two?" Danny asked. He stood so close to Shirley, their shoulders touched.

"One can only hope," Suzanne said.

"Did your ex get back to you?" Tom said, rising from his chair.

"He tried."

"Well, call him again. I'll get some clearer captures from the video and can either send them directly to him or to you so you can forward them on. If he's the one who studies these kinds of things, he'll know for sure."

Simon DiNardo spoke up in a voice that couldn't be ignored. "I think this is above our pay grade. We're not out here to discover new species of fish. And one of our primary tools for studying what we are paid to do is now sitting at the bottom of the goddamn ocean. We need to park ourselves in the nearest port and report what happened. I don't know what the hell those things are, but if they're not impacting the climate, I honestly don't give a damn."

"They're not impacting the climate," Suzanne repeated. She walked in a slow circle around the bridge.

Cranky Simon was on to something.

"Maybe," she said, all eyes on her, "it's the other way around. Maybe it's the climate that's affecting them."

"I think that's stretching things," Simon said, folding his arms across his chest.

Suzanne held up a hand, still pacing. "Hear me out. We know that frozen methane is often released when water temperatures rise just enough to melt a fraction of the ice its been encapsulated within. You do agree that part is within our pay grade, right?"

Simon's face remained unreadable.

"What if those things were frozen in the ice along with the methane?" she said.

Slowly and with the condescending tone of a father talking to an idiot child, Simon said, "This is not a B-movie, Suzanne. Should we look for a couple of tiny Japanese women to call on a giant butterfly to help us out?"

Jabbing at the image on the monitor, Suzanne even startled herself by yelling, "Just look at that! They're coming *out* of the fissure! It's like they're being thawed, revived and released. They exist, Simon. We're not looking at a reel someone smuggled in from the drive-in. Just yesterday we all saw what those same fish did to those men. That one guy was crushed thinner than a pamphlet. And now the same thing happened to *Badass*. If we didn't think it could happen to us, we'd be back there right now trying to retrieve it."

"Look, I'm not denying these things exist," Simon said, raising his hands. "I'm just saying let's follow the rules, whatever the hell they are in this kind of situation, and leave the fish stuff to people who know better."

Tom put a gentle hand on her shoulder.

"Maybe we all need to just step back for a bit and give our minds a chance to wrap around everything. Until then, I'll call the Coast Guard and tell them what happened."

Shirley gave a nervous laugh. "Yeah, maybe they can go over there and blast them back to wherever they came from."

"They're the Coast Guard, not the Navy," Danny said.

"Then they can call in the Navy," she said.

"We all know how much they love to work with each other."

Coast Guard and Navy scuffles were well known and legendary. Their stance against one another went beyond good-natured ribbing. Suzanne got an earful about it when she dated a cute guy in the Navy with a jawline that should have been set in bronze for future generations to admire. They referred to the Guard as the Fisher Price Navy, on account of the scut work they did being akin to child's play.

"Tom's right, I think we all just need to settle down," Shirley said.

And I'm right, too, she thought. *We're going to have to be a part of this.*

Walking to the stern, she tried Whit again and got his voicemail.

"Whit, it's Suzanne again. Things are getting serious over here. I know you're on another continent and my voice isn't exactly the one you want to hear, but I need you to get back to me right away. Please, Whit. I wouldn't be pestering you if it wasn't serious."

Ending the call, Suzanne leaned against the industrial winch used to lower and retrieve *Badass* from the water. She turned her face into the salty breeze. Her scarlet locks looked like a nest of angry, hyperactive snakes.

For the first time in years, she wished Whit were here with her.

THIRTEEN

"There's nothing here," Whit said. He leaned over Travis Hewitt's shoulder, studying the fish finder. The *SenoRita* had all the bells and whistles a spanking new fishing boat could boast, and he was grateful. When he fished, he always felt fish finders were cheating. In this case, he'd take any advantage he could get.

"Not if you're fishing for grouper," Travis said. "A lot of fish dinners being pulled up right now."

The *SenoRita* rocked amidst a sector of the Atlantic dotted with other party fishing boats. The boats were crammed with mostly men, poles in hand, mates busy running back and forth with their nets.

Whit turned to look outside the pilothouse when he heard Nestor heave another gutful into the ocean.

"You okay back there?"

There was a pause, then the sound of Nestor hocking up wads of spit. "I think that's the last of it. I swear I just saw the pernil I ate three nights ago."

Jim Hewitt was below on the bow, his hands wrapped around high-powered binoculars. Whit had asked him to be on the lookout for anyone reeling up an oversized chimaera fish.

"What's a chimaera fish look like?" he'd asked, tying a wet bandanna on his head to keep cool and guard against the sun's powerful rays. Skin cancer was all too common for people who worked the ocean. When Whit showed him the pictures he'd taken of the one caught in this same area, the kid pulled a face.

"That's not real, right?"

In the picture, one of the volunteers at the University was standing next to the table on which the giant fish lay for perspective.

"Do meth heads have dental issues?" Whit said. "There are more of those puppies out here. I need to find out how many and why they're so far from home."

Jim's Adam's apple bobbed and he asked no more questions. It was easy to see he was none too thrilled knowing something like that could be just below them. He'd been vigilant ever since.

The boat's fish finder was top of the line. Sonar devices could be purchased at a Wal-Mart by weekend fishermen, but few had one this good. The finder on the *SenoRita* had to cost a few thousand bucks. It was like looking at the ocean in the clear light of day – up to a certain depth, at least.

"Come on, give me something to dive in for," Whit said to the finder's display the way a gambler would urge a horse to take the lead on the far turn.

Travis stifled a burp and said, "You mind if I ask you a question?"

"Ask away."

The waves lapped against the side of the boat, a cool ocean breeze filling the cabin. For the first time since stepping off the plane at Miami International Airport, Whit felt completely at ease. His mother warned him he'd become a fish some day, like Don Knotts in *The Incredible Mr. Limpet*. Maybe she was right.

"If this thing is big enough and dangerous enough to kill a man, why are you so hopped up to meet it face-to-face?" Travis said.

"It's kinda my job. I've been studying chimaera fish for years. When something like this comes along, I don't know. I just have to see it for myself in its natural environment." Whit scratched at his two-day beard. "I've been told I'm not the brightest bulb in the pack."

"If those fish can do what you say, without teeth, I'm inclined to agree."

Whit laughed, expecting Travis to at least break a smile. The man went back to checking the boat's navigation system and engine monitors.

Okay, he thinks I'm nuts.

Stepping outside to check on Nestor, the bright sun caused him to squint until his eyes were almost closed.

"Don't say 'I told you so'," Nestor preempted. "On hindsight, I should have bought some Dramamine."

Whit clapped him on the back. "The good news is that once you hit empty, the rest is smooth sailing, so to speak."

The boat rocked from starboard to port, and Whit stumbled. The lower pocket of his cargo shorts clanged off the handrail.

"And now I've broken my phone," he sighed, pulling it from his pocket so he could inspect the damage. To his relief, the screen wasn't cracked. He went through phones the way he could plow through margaritas. He saw that there were more messages from Suzanne. Opening his voicemail, he put the phone on speaker. She sounded very upset.

"*I know you're on another continent and my voice isn't exactly the one you want to hear, but I need you to get back to me right away. Please, Whit. I wouldn't be pestering you if it wasn't serious.*"

"She's wrong about two things," he said.

"What's that?" Nestor said.

"I'm a lot closer than she thinks. And despite our past, I actually like hearing her voice." He always did. It was his voice, many times slurred, that tended to irritate Suzanne.

But not like this, he thought. Suzanne had never been big on emotion. He used to joke around when they were married, introducing them as Fire and Ice. She hated when he did it, and like a man-child, he never could stop himself.

That ice sounds like it's thawed considerably.

He dialed her number, hoping he didn't get voicemail this time. He hated leaving messages on voicemail. He'd always felt like an idiot talking to a machine, knowing if he said something dumb or awkward, it was recorded, a captured history of his verbal blunders. Of course, there was less chance of putting his foot in his mouth now when he was stone-cold sober.

To his surprise, she picked up on the first ring.

"Whit?"

He froze for a moment, unsure what to say next. This was a woman who knew everything about him, the good and the bad, a lot of it bad when they were together. Why was he tongue-tied?

"Uh, hey Suzie, I know we've been playing phone tag..."

She cut him off.

"I have someone sending you video right now," she said.

"What?"

Someone screamed something in the background.

"They're attacking our ship," she said.

A lump burned in his throat.

"Who's attacking your ship?" he blurted louder than he intended.

"I'm not sure. We're maneuvering away from them now, but they're fast."

"Suze, you're not making any sense."

"You can help us by watching the video."

The rapid beat of air blowing in the phone's microphone made it hard to hear her. She must be on the deck.

"I will. I will. Where are you?"

The connection started to disintegrate.

"Suzie? Suzie? Give me your coordinates. I'm in Miami. I can come to you. Suzie?"

There was static, and then she was gone. Whit gripped the phone, tempted to launch it into the ocean.

The video.

Several had been sent to his email.

"Are you okay?" Nestor said.

Whit sat down heavily, cradling the phone in his hands, waiting for the first video to load.

He couldn't get past the fear in Suzanne's voice. He'd call her right back, hope for a solid connection.

The video started. At first there was nothing but bubbles obscuring the view. As they cleared, he saw what had put Suzanne in such a state.

Without looking up, he said, "No, Nestor, I'm as far from fucking okay as I've ever been."

FOURTEEN

The first inclination that they were under attack was a series of hard thumps on the hull of the *Porpoise IV*. Everyone felt them as much as heard them. First there was one, followed by two quick knocks, as if Poseidon was politely asking to be let inside the boat.

It quickly became a steady pounding, a hailstorm from the deep. Suzanne and Shirley rushed to the rail on the stern to see if they could spot what was slamming into them.

Both yelped with shock when they saw several dark shapes the size of Beluga whales swimming close to the surface, slipping under the *Porpoise IV*. One or several of the fish hit it so hard, the survey vessel canted portside for a breathless second.

"We have to get the hell out of here!" Suzanne shouted, running to the bridge. "It's those same fish by the methane vent."

Ken Beekman didn't need to be told. He already had the turbo diesel engine humming. Their max speed was only sixteen knots, but beggars couldn't be choosers.

"I thought we'd put those damn things behind us," Ken said through gritted teeth. If he was scared, he didn't show it. Knowing him, he was more concerned about the fish damaging the ship.

"We all thought so," Tom said sharply.

As the *Porpoise IV* gathered speed, heading west and further from the methane vent and its population of aggressive, oversized fish, one of the creatures leapt from the water like a dolphin right off the bow.

Suzanne's assessment that the fish below were the size of Beluga whales had been close. In fact, they were longer, though not quite as thick around. The fish slammed into the water, just

62

missing landing on the deck. A tremendous splash of ocean brine rained down on the ship.

"I'll be damned," Ken said, piloting right over the spot where the fish dove.

"That's an understatement," Suzanne said.

Once the ship hit full speed and the horrendous thumping was behind them, she dared to venture outside again. Her phone rang. When she saw it was Whit, she was quick to answer it. Hearing his voice restored some of her resolve. These things had to be Whit's fish, though mutated in some way. He'd know what to do.

In the middle of her telling him to watch the videos Tom had sent, the call broke apart.

She thought she heard him say he was in Miami, though she couldn't be sure, and something about coordinates.

He definitely said Miami *and* coordinates. *Why would our coordinates matter? Unless there's a chance he's actually nearby!*

Texting him back to let him know their approximate position, she didn't notice Danny Garza beside her. He was pretty shaken up.

"Please tell me that didn't just happen," he said. His eyes were glassy, unfocused.

"I wish I could," she replied, correcting the typing mistakes she kept making because her fingers were so unsteady.

Suzanne didn't pay attention to Danny until she heard the explosion of water and the young man's scream.

One of the fish had managed to keep up with the ship's retreat. It had burst from the surface, its mouth wrapped around Danny's arm, tugging him overboard to certain death.

The call for 'man overboard' brought everyone scrambling to the deck. Suzanne did her best to stay calm enough to explain what had happened.

"It jumped up and just grabbed him?" Simon said, hanging over the rail and gazing at the passing waters. "We have to tell Ken to stop!"

"We can't," Suzanne said. "We have to put as much distance as we can from those things, if that's even possible. And stay away from the rail!"

"Are you sure he didn't just fall over?"

The boat rocked at that moment, and Simon skidded in the slick pool of Danny's blood, falling onto his side. Several hands reached out to help him up, but not before he was coated red.

"Oh my God, oh my God!"

Tom held Shirley. The moment she saw the blood, she knew. Tom was the only thing keeping her upright.

"We have to get off the deck," Suzanne said, pointing to the elevated bridge. "It's not safe down here."

Shirley broke from Tom's grasp, leaping for the rail, calling out Danny's name, tears spluttering from her mouth. Suzanne grabbed her by the shoulders, pulling her back with strength she didn't know she possessed.

The woman's head moved out of the way of a leaping fish, its mouth clamping shut on empty air before tumbling back into the sea. Even Simon cried out in terror.

Suzanne didn't need to tell everyone twice to get the hell away. The men made sure the women took the small flight of steps first. She gripped the handrails as hard as she could. With the ship going at full speed, swaying from starboard to port, she didn't want to fall from the steps and into the churning water.

Once everyone was on the outdoor observation deck on the bridge, they could clearly see the humped shapes in pursuit of the *Porpoise IV*.

"Holy mother of…how many of those damn things are out there?" Tom said, eyes so wide, it looked as if he'd been zapped by a cattle prod.

Suzanne tried to count, but it was impossible to get an accurate number. "Maybe twenty or more near the surface, but who the hell knows how many more are just out of sight.

"They must think *Badass* was an appetizer," Simon said, one long-fingered hand over his mouth. "Now they want the main course." The man looked as if he'd stepped out of an abattoir. The sharp, old penny tang of Danny's blood made Suzanne's stomach cringe.

Shirley's sobs hadn't abated. "I can't. I can't," she mumbled before heading inside.

"Poor Danny," Tom said.

Suzanne could see Danny's face, twisted in pain and stark dread, moments before the impossible fish ripped him from his feet. She would never forget his screams for as long as she lived, or the wet, tearing sound his arm made as it was partially separate from his body.

"We gotta call this in," Simon said, heading inside the bridge.

It didn't happen often, but Simon was right. This was a job for the Navy. They needed to blast these abominations right out of the water. Suzanne shivered. She'd been anti-gun and anti-war all her life.

She never imagined a force like this, a class of cold, emotionless fish that through their size and fervor to destroy anything they see, could make the ocean waters the most dangerous place in the world.

Raymond Basu, who spent most of his time belowdecks in front of his computers, tapped Suzanne on the shoulder. She could smell the shaving cream scent that lingered over his freshly shorn face and head. He was fastidious about shaving, even more so when he was stressed. With his dark skin and creased flesh on the top of his dome, he resembled a walnut. They'd sailed into a few storms together over the years, his walnut getting the razor treatment twice in a day if the seas were really bad.

"What's Shirley doing?" Raymond said.

Shirley popped into view below them. She was headed straight for the stern, right where the fish were doing their damnedest to keep up with the ship. Suzanne saw the gun in her hand and shouted, "Shirley, no!"

Pop! Pop!

The first two shots made small splashes in the water.

"Where the hell did she get a gun?" Tom said, running alongside Suzanne to pull Shirley away.

She didn't need to tell him that Shirley grew up and still lived in a dicey part of Atlanta. Carrying a gun was as normal to her as having her wallet and makeup in her pocketbook. Suzanne had once asked her why she didn't move, now that she had the capital to get her ass to a better, safer area.

"It's my Dad," she'd said. "He's all alone and his home is his world. I can't leave him."

They hit the main deck the moment Shirley ripped off a succession of shots.

One of them must have hit home, because a fish over twenty feet long bounded from the ocean, falling backwards. The bullets coming out of her .38 couldn't kill something that big, only irritate it.

In response, a trio of smaller fish went airborne, heading straight for Shirley.

FIFTEEN

To his credit, Travis Hewitt didn't even ask a single question when Whit told him they had to make their way east into deeper water. He merely said, "You're the captain on this three-hour tour. I'm just the guy who drives the boat."

He gave Travis the coordinates that Suzanne had texted over, which the grizzled man entered into his computer. The boat shifted course immediately.

"They're probably on the move, so we won't find them at that exact spot, but maybe we can intercept them," Whit said.

Travis arched an eyebrow. "Sure. There's always a chance."

They both knew how small that chance was. The ocean's size was too much for a person to completely fathom. If they were off by merely one degree, both ships would have an iceberg's chance in Texas of seeing one another.

Nestor stumbled into the pilothouse. He'd gone from green to pale, which was a good sign.

"Where are we going?" he said.

They watched the party fishing boats turn to small dots in the retreating distance.

Whit said, "I'm sorry Nestor, but we're heading out deeper into the ocean. My wife, I mean my ex-wife, is on a climatology research vessel. It looks like they spotted the same fish I've been looking for, except these fish are highly aggressive."

Travis eased off the throttle. He narrowed his gaze at Whit. "Now hold on a second. What do you mean by aggressive? And how big are these things? If we come across them, what are we going to do, smack 'em to death with some fishing poles?"

Taking a deep breath, Whit said, "We'll burn that bridge when we get to it."

"Or destroy my boat in the process."

"I think that would be highly unlikely."

At least I hope it is, Whit thought.

He added, "Look, if anything happens to the *SenoRita*, the company I work for will gladly pay for it. If these things are what I think they are, they're the find of the century, hell, of any century. If people thought discovering a living coelacanth was big news, they're about to have their world turned upside down."

"What the heck is a coelacanth?" Nestor asked.

"A fish that was believed to have gone extinct millions of years ago," Whit said. "That is until one was caught in the 30s. Goes to show we're not always right."

"Are they as ugly as your fish?" Nestor said.

"Not quite, but they'll never win a Miss America contest."

These chimaera fish were unlike any other even found in the fossil record. When word got out, marine biology as a major study was about to take a quantum leap, the way rocket science fascinated young students in the 50s and 60s.

Travis didn't appear to share his enthusiasm. The boat was still headed in the right direction, but at a much slower pace.

"Look," Whit added, "they could be in trouble. We can't leave people out there if they need our help."

Travis snickered. "That's what the damn Coast Guard is for. I was asked to help you find a fish that could scare away the fishing trade, not be a white knight for a research vessel you *think* is in trouble."

Whit was about to outright plead when Jim Hewitt said, "Dad, we shouldn't ignore this." He had Whit's cell phone in his hands. Whit barely remembered setting it down on one of the chairs when he came in. Jim was playing one of the videos that had been sent to Whit. It was the one where the giant chimaera attacked the submersible. "You have to see this."

Taking a moment to stare hard into each man's eyes, Travis reluctantly took the phone from his son. He watched it, his expression stolid throughout.

After the video ended, he looked up at Whit. "This can't be real."

"My ex wouldn't lie. She's a climatologist and spends half her life on the ocean. She's seen a lot of shit. This has her scared."

As well it should, he neglected to add.

"Hard to tell how big they are from that," Travis said.

"Big enough to rock the ship they're on. Big enough to swarm a fishing trawler and kill the crew," Whit said.

"And too big to run away from," Nestor added. All eyes went to him. He shrugged. "I don't know how I can help, but I'm willing to try. If you say your ex-wife and her crew are in danger, we have a moral responsibility to help them."

That was the clincher. Whit knew that Travis wouldn't allow himself to be accused of cowardice by a landlubber. Especially not one who had just seasoned the ocean with his stomach.

Finally, Travis said, "Try to get ahold of your ex. Find out the name of her ship. I'm calling this in to the Coast Guard on the way. You and Julie May are going to owe me big time for this one."

"It's the *Porpoise IV*, unless things have changed," Whit replied. The *Porpoise IV* was where she'd actually moved into when they first split up, leaving him their apartment that neither used much toward the end.

Easing the throttle forward, Travis took the *SenoRita* to full speed.

Whit leaned against the wall and prayed they'd find Suzanne before something happened to her.

"Hey," he called out to Travis. "You got anything to drink?"

"I assume you don't mean water."

"You're a world class assumer."

Even it was just a sip, Whit needed that burn to settle his roiling gut.

Travis lifted up his seat. He pulled a half-full bottle of bourbon out from the storage area and tossed it to Whit. "Save some for me when this is over. I never drive drunk, but I also don't like to sit around sober."

Whit tipped the bottle toward him in thanks, then took a quick drag. He asked Nestor if he wanted some, but the man politely and unsurprisingly refused.

"You shouldn't drink too much," Nestor warned.

"Don't worry," Whit said, tipping the bottle back again. "There's not enough in here to come close to my version of too much."

Suzanne, Raymond and Tom got to Shirley at the same time. Three hands grabbed various parts of her clothing, yanking her backward.

Two of the leaping fish came up short, their cold black eyes boring into them for an instant before disappearing from view.

But one of them made a stronger dive for the ship. Its head slammed onto the deck, right where Shirley had been standing. The *Porpoise IV* tilted back for a terrifying moment, the weight of the mammoth fish tipping the scales.

They fell on their rumps, sliding toward its great, open mouth.

"Hold on!" Suzanne shrieked, reaching out for a thick rope to stop their slide. As they were all still holding onto Shirley, she had to bear the weight of four people. Her shoulder was close to dislocating. Biting her lip until it bled, she tightened her grip on the collar of Shirley's shirt.

The fish's mouth slammed shut with a wet smack that rattled Suzanne's ribcage.

An impossibly long instant later, the head reared back as the fish flopped back into the ocean. The railing was demolished, the wood of the deck splintered.

The moment it was gone, they scrambled to their feet and back on the upper observation deck. Whatever psychosis had compelled Shirley to take potshots at the creatures appeared to have dissipated. She urged them to move faster when they hit the stairs.

"What the hell were you thinking?" Simon barked, hands on his hips, glaring at them incredulously.

Shirley turned on him. "They killed Danny, you impotent motherfucker!"

Suzanne had to hold her back from taking a swing at the crew's resident curmudgeon.

"You could have gotten us all killed, you crazy bitch!" Simon roared, turning his back to them and storming off before Shirley could retort.

Suzanne stroked the woman's hair while Raymond wrapped his arms around her. She struggled for a bit, then relented to Suzanne's soft yet firm command to calm down.

"Screw Simon," Shirley sputtered, going limp, her grief and rage seeping from her charged nerves.

Suzanne cradled her face in her hands, their noses inches apart. "Look, I need you to promise me that you're going to hold yourself together. Simon's not my favorite person in the world, but he was right. You saw how close that thing got to us. What if it crippled the ship? We'd be dead by now."

Eyes shimmering with tears, Shirley nodded. "I'm done. I promise. No more outbursts. I kinda lost my shit for a moment."

"Kinda," Raymond repeated with a hint of sarcasm. Suzanne motioned for him to let Shirley go.

"Why don't you go wash up and take a break?" Suzanne said. Shirley left without saying another word.

She mouthed to Raymond – *why don't you keep an eye on her?*

She hadn't noticed that Tom had gone into the pilothouse with Simon. He came out now, clapping his hands together. "Ken says he got a call from a fishing boat not far from us."

"So?" Suzanne said.

"Your ex is on that boat. They'll meet up with us barring any more disasters within an hour or so."

She leaned against the railing, looking out over the stern. The pursuing phantoms were no longer in sight. Maybe that had been their last gasp. Coming up empty-handed was enough for them to seek easier prey.

"Whit's here?"

"It appears so. I know you wanted his advice, but are you okay with seeing him face to face? I can always have Ken tell them we're heading for shore and you can sneak off before he gets ahold of you."

Tom had been there when things went bad – the drinking, the fights, long stretches of time spent apart with neither heart growing fonder for the other. He'd been her sounding board for so long, she knew he had a very one-sided view of Whit. There had been good times, too. It was just hard to remember when she was in the middle of the worst times.

"No, I'll be fine. It's just kinda weird to know he's here. I think the closest we've been to one another was a year and a half ago when I was working out of Johannesburg and he was in New Zealand."

"Okay, but if you need me, I'll be here." Shielding his eyes from the sun, Tom said, "Well, I think we finally outran them. It's a miracle the stern held up. Between that and *Badass*, we're going to have to do some extreme budget begging to get our gear back up to speed."

Feeling as if she could finally relax even just a little, Suzanne took several long, deep breaths. The fresh sea air was a miracle when it came to cleansing her system.

"I'll worry about the begging later. Right now, we have to figure out what the hell is going on."

SIXTEEN

The *SenoRita* met up with the *Porpoise IV* just as the sun was beginning to dip below the horizon. The water turned darker while the sky purpled, pink striations hovering over the setting orange orb.

The first thing they noticed was the damage to the ship's stern.

"Looks like someone rear-ended them good," Travis said. "Hope they got his insurance."

Whit stalked out of the pilothouse. He heard Nestor ask, "Was that supposed to be funny?" Followed by an exasperated huff by Travis.

Whit felt jittery, more nervous about seeing Suzanne again than the killer fish stalking the ocean.

As the *SenoRita* pulled alongside the research vessel, Suzanne's head popped over the railing. She looked as if she hadn't slept in days. Her eyes were rimmed by dark circles and her face seemed pinched, as if she were holding something deep inside lest it shatter her usual calm demeanor.

"Is that really you?" she said.

He released a breath he wasn't even aware he'd been holding. A part of him expected Suzanne to hurl a few choice invectives his way. Asking for his help on the phone was one thing. Seeing him in person might awaken all that anger she'd justifiably had toward him.

"Either that or a very good looking body-double," he called up to her.

"You're going gray."

"Better that than bald."

A hint of a smile played on her lips.

"You have something I can use to get aboard?" he asked.

She moved out of view, replaced by Tom Mitchelson.

"Hey, Tom. It's been a while."

"I think you puked on my pants last time I saw you," he said, his face unreadable.

Whit thought about it, unable to recall the event. Blackouts could be a good thing.

"I've puked on a lot of pants, Tom. Some say it's good luck." He beamed a smile back at him.

Remember not to elect Tom president of my fan club, he thought, almost laughing out loud. That would not have made an awkward situation any easier.

"Here," Suzanne said, tossing a rope ladder over the side of the *Porpoise IV*. "Think an old man like you can manage it?"

"Never judge a book by its hair."

Whit waited until the boats were close enough for him to leap off the rail, snatching the cords of the ladder. It wasn't the smartest or easiest way to do it, but Whit always preferred the road less traveled. Glancing back at Nestor, he said, "You guys stay put. I'll be back in a few."

Nestor looked relieved not to have to jump between ships.

Suzanne and Tom helped him climb aboard.

"Who's the guy with the fedora?" Suzanne asked.

Whit had to take a moment before answering. She still looked damn good. Exhausted, but beautiful as ever.

"That's Nestor. He started as my chauffeur, and he's since been elevated to *guy who can get shit done*."

"It's good to have a guy like that," she said, waving at Nestor, who waved back, his pearly teeth cutting through the coming darkness.

"Tom," Whit said, shaking the man's hand.

"Never thought we'd see you here," Tom said.

"Fate has its act together," Whit replied.

"No thanks to your fish."

"Why do people keep calling them my fish?"

He opened his arms, and Suzanne and he made a quick, stiff embrace.

"It's good to see you, Suze."

And in one piece, he thought.

"Believe it or not, it's good to see you, too," she said. "If we had a fat guy in a red suit nearby, we could call it a Christmas miracle."

Whit chuckled. "This is the Bermuda Triangle. Anything's possible." Looking toward the ruined stern, he said, "What happened back there?"

Suzanne said, "Follow me. I'll introduce you to everyone and give you the rundown."

He noticed crimson stains on the port deck. "And that?"

A cloud settled over her face, and she visibly stiffened. "We lost one of our crew today. It was...horrible. We're all still in shock."

"Jesus."

As they walked, Tom said, "Don't blame him. What's been happening comes from a little further south."

Whit met the small crew, all of them looking worse for wear. One of them, an older guy named Simon, didn't even bother to shake his hand, choosing instead to mutter something before stalking off. It looked like there were flecks of dried blood near his hairline. He also noted that the girl with the Mohawk, Shirley, had obviously been crying earlier.

All signs that things had not gone well.

He heard over the communications system that a Coast Guard cutter was en route. Everyone aboard the *Porpoise IV* sagged with relief.

"God bless the cavalry," Tom said. Looking to Whit, he motioned for him to take a seat by a bank of monitors. "While Suzanne fills you in on what's happened, I'll show you the video we captured."

"I'm in Miami because a record-sized chimaera fish supposedly killed a mate on a fishing boat with its venom," Whit said.

"Did they catch the fish?" Suzanne asked, taking the seat next to him.

"They did and I've since dissected it. It was a chimaera fish, that's for sure. I have a friend running toxicology on the man's blood and the samples I took from the fish. You remember

Garrett? Nestor was able to get a boat so I could go out and see if there were more of them about. What you had sent me confirmed that we're dealing with something that's gonna change the old paradigm," Whit said, watching the video taken from their submersible. "And it's exceedingly dangerous, just in case that wasn't enough."

Pointing at the monitor, Suzanne said, "That's a methane vent we were out investigating. It's one of the biggest we've ever come across in the Atlantic. You'll see the big surprise in just a few seconds."

When the school of chimaera fish came into focus, darting in and out and around the crack in the ocean floor, Whit leaned so far forward, his nose almost touched the screen. He couldn't believe what he was seeing.

"It looks like they're coming from that rupture," he said.

"That's what we think, too," Tom said.

There were so many of them.

"They destroyed our sub," Suzanne said. "And subsequently attacked our ship. They chased us for miles." She told him everything that had happened, from the creatures hurling themselves at the hull like cudgels, to Danny Garza being pulled overboard and nearly being demolished after Shirley's attempt to shoot one.

Whit's head spun.

"Wait," he said, rubbing his temples. "You said they were how big?"

Suzanne drew a fluttery breath. Her fingers tapped on the table. *She's jonesing for a cigarette*, Whit thought.

"I'd estimate the biggest one we saw so far had to be the one that slammed into the stern. It had to be twenty, twenty-three feet in length."

"That's impossible," Whit said. "The largest I'd ever seen until this past week was under four feet. I can buy a mutation topping out at six feet, but twenty?"

Shirley stood behind them. Whit saw she had a tattoo of a Celtic knot on one of her wrists. "You think something smaller could have done that damage?"

He wanted to challenge them, insinuate that they'd been attacked by something else and merely thought it was a chimaera because of their recent run-in. Was there a chance they were chased by a pod of orcas? Their distinctive features would have made it very hard to confuse them with a chimaera, a fish aptly referred to as a ghost shark. Some chimaera fish could very much look as if they came from another dimension.

No one spoke for a while.

Rising from her seat, Suzanne said, "Why don't you come outside with me?"

It was hard to miss the warning glance he received from Tom as he followed her out of the pilothouse. Was she sleeping with him? He'd suspected it back when they first broke up. Or had he appointed himself her protector, especially when it came to all things Whit?

The night air was cool and crisp. He saw lights in the distance, wondering if it was the Coast Guard.

"You need a coffin nail?" he asked her. She hugged her arms around herself, giving a slight shiver.

"I'd kill for one."

Whit called down to the *SenoRita*. "Hey, Travis, any chance you have some smokes?"

The fishing boat captain came out holding a pack of cigarettes. "I'll add that to my tab," Travis said. He tossed them up to Whit, the breeze nearly sweeping the box out to sea. Whit took a couple, then flipped the pack back to him.

Suzanne reached into her pocket. "I have a lighter."

"Always the girl scout."

She lit one, tucking the other behind her ear.

"I watched that boy get swallowed up by one of those things, Whit. It grabbed his arm and I could hear it just…pop."

When he reached out to hold her, she took a step back. "I'm never going to be able to forget that sound, or the way he looked at me just before it dragged him over. How the hell is all of this even possible?"

He shook his head. "I'm as confused as you all are, maybe more so because I know these fish like the back of my hand. Or like the back of your hand at one time."

She softened ever so slightly.

"I have a theory, but it's pretty out there," she said, taking a long drag. Smoke billowed from her mouth in twisting tendrils, pulled apart by the sea breeze.

"Ever since I landed in Miami, everything has been out there."

She walked the deck, careful to stay away from the rail.

In starts and stops, she talked about the possibility that the chimaera fish had been encased in ice and methane. Now that the oceans were warming and the ice melting, they were being set free – two destructive forces best left below the ocean floor.

"If that's the case," Whit said, looking down at the bobbing *SenoRita*, "the chimaeras are older than any we've ever found in the fossil record. We're talking ten million or more years older than we initially thought them to be. My head hurts just thinking about it. I know fish can lower their metabolic rate in icy waters to survive, but total suspended animation for millennia? It makes no scientific sense."

Suzanne jabbed at the air with the cigarette between her fingers. "Okay, say they weren't trapped in the ice. Maybe they're attracted to the methane."

"A fish that enjoys a hearty breakfast of methane?" Whit covered his face with his hands, eyes closed tight. "Impossible."

"People thought sea life would be impossible around thermal vents, but now we know areas we were damn sure were uninhabitable can not only bring about life, but sustain it. You've said it yourself to me time and time again – we know so little about the sea, we're like toddlers trying to explain the planetary balance of our solar system."

Whit looked at her over his fingertips, one eyebrow cocked. "I said that?"

Suzanne nodded. "More times than I can count. You liked to pontificate late at night, or early in the morning, usually when I was trying to get some sleep."

He wanted to apologize, but what was the point? The damage was already done.

"I may have been a pain in the ass, but I was right," he said.

To his surprise, she grabbed hold of his arms, her eyes locked on his. "Then open your mind and let what you see lead you to the truth. You're a pain in the ass, but you're good at what you do and just crazy enough to find the truth."

Savoring her touch, he stared back at a moonlit face that once peered back at him just one pillow away. She must have sensed the wellspring of feelings bubbling up between them, breaking away and turning to face the battered stern. He looked up at the brilliant splashes of stars, some clusters so dense, they were like nightlights in a darkened bedroom.

After a while, he said, "There is a way we can test your theory."

She turned to face him.

Whit said, "We go to the next three biggest methane vents in the area. If we find them there, we know there's a solid connection."

"But we lost our sub. How will we be able to see them?"

"If they're as big as you said, they'll be hard to miss."

SEVENTEEN

Nestor's heart thumped when he saw the Coast Guard cutter pull into view. He gave silent thanks to Jesus, Mary and any saint who would listen.

Travis was at the bow, a fishing line in the water, the orange tip of a cigar casting meager light on his tanned face. He brought the binoculars up to his eyes.

"Here comes *The Black Jack* to the rescue," Travis said, letting the binoculars fall to his chest. "I used to go on those damn floating casinos out in international waters. Never did win. Let's hope we're luckier this time."

The single-masted ship turned on several bright spotlights, sweeping over the *SenoRita* and *Porpoise IV*. It was one of the smaller vessels the Guard deployed, but it was fast.

Nestor looked at the fishing pole in Travis's hands and said, "You really think you should be fishing when those things are down there?"

Travis gave a derisive snort. "You don't fish, do you?"

"I used to fish with my uncles on a lake in upstate New York when I was a kid."

Sweeping his hand over the oceanic tableau, Travis said, "As you can see, this isn't a lake. Those fish we saw on Whit's phone wouldn't have any interest in the meager bait I have on this line. Now, if I were to somehow hook a big fella like you, well, things might get interesting."

Stepping back, Nestor said, "Are you threatening me?"

Exploding with laughter, Travis had to lock the pole in a holder and hold his sides. "You got me! I set this whole thing up so I could feed a man to a killer fish. Do you drink?"

"Occasionally," Nestor said, his flash of panic gone and looking sillier by the second.

"You need to do it more often, relax a little."

Rubbing his hands together to ward off a chill that wasn't there, Nestor said, "I'm finding that a little hard out here in the middle of the ocean at night."

The Coast Guard cutter was so close, they could hear the churning of the water and break in the chop. "And for some reason, that's not making me feel any easier," Nestor added, pointing at the sleek yet powerful ship. Were things so bad they needed to bring in ships with guns? The presence of the Coast Guard should have calmed his fears, not added to them.

"You regretting you didn't stay on the dock?"

He pondered it for a bit, then said, "Actually, no. I spent most of my life playing things safe. It'd be nice to have a little adventure to tell my grandkids about."

"I'm sure the missus will be impressed."

Taking a breath, Nestor said, "She passed away a couple of years ago. I've been trying to keep my mind busy ever since. It's partly why I've been so eager to help Whit."

Travis squeezed his shoulder. "I'm sorry to hear that. My wife left me and Jimmy five years ago. I see her only once or twice a year, but I still think I'd be in sorry shape if she passed tomorrow."

Both men stiffened at the echo of heavy thumping against metal.

"What the hell is that?" Nestor said, grabbing for the nearest handrail.

"Jim?" Travis called up to the pilothouse.

"I'm on it," his son shouted.

Travis and Nestor bolted up the stairs. Reverberating thuds, as alien as a giant's footfalls, thrummed repeatedly. Travis turned on the fish finder while Jim flipped on the big searchlight.

"Holy Christ," Travis groaned. "They're everywhere."

The fish finder's screen was filled with fast moving shapes, most of them a quarter the size of the *SenoRita*.

"Is it those fish?" Nestor said, unable to hide the rising panic in his voice.

"I can't tell for sure, hold on."

Travis angled next to his son, taking over the searchlight. The big fish were swimming just under them, but they weren't hitting into the *SenoRita* or *Porpoise IV*. He concentrated the beam's light on the cutter. Jim gasped as one of the beastly fish broke the surface in a great spray, ramming its head into the side of the cutter. The ocean around the cutter was alive with chimaera fish, hell-bent on pounding the rock-solid ship like a coke-fueled drummer.

"Nestor!"

He popped his head out the window. Whit was at the rail of the Porpoise IV. "Tell Travis to get the hell out of here while they're distracted. Don't hold back!"

"What about you?"

"I'll be fine onboard here. Just go now!"

From the moment he'd met him, the marine biologist – no, ichthyologist – seemed about as calm a person as he'd ever met. The wild look in Whit's eyes now chilled him.

"Whit says…"

"Yeah, I'm already on it. Hold on," Travis barked.

The engine thundered and they banked hard, away from the *Porpoise IV*. Nestor stumbled, crashing into a wall. Jim held on to the searchlight, not letting the attacking fish out of his sight.

The *Porpoise IV* groaned to life, heading in the opposite direction.

"Holy shit. Look at them," Jim said.

Water frothed around the cutter as the giant chimaera fish swarmed it like killer bees. Nestor grabbed the binoculars. Several managed to flop on board. Nestor could only imagine what the men were thinking as the fish snapped at anyone on the deck. The staccato of small arms fire rode above the pounding of the fish on the ship. In the searchlight's ovular beam, they could see men running to the rails, taking aim at the diving beasts. Bullets hit their mark but didn't seem to have any effect.

There were sharp screams. Nestor's bowels liquefied as he watched the shadows of men crushed under falling chimaera bodies, while others were ensnared in their massive jaws.

"It's like looking at the gates of hell," he whispered.

It seemed weak and shameful to leave the Coast Guard, but they had a vastly superior ship and guns. What could the *SenoRita* do to help?

They pulled away from the melee as fast as the fishing boat would take them.

"Some of them are coming this way!" Jim shouted. He kept the light on the undulating bodies swimming close to the surface, blazing through the *SenoRita's* wake.

"Dammit!" Travis snapped. He looked down at the fish finder. "Got a bunch of them changing course. They must be attracted to movement in the dark."

"Maybe we should just stop, then," Nestor said.

"It's too late," Travis said, grinding his cigarette between his teeth. "They've got our scent. I'm going to have to try and outrun them."

Jim radioed the *Porpoise IV*. "SenoRita to *Porpoise IV*. Mayday. We're being pursued by the chimaera fish. They may be attracted by movement. Cut your engine if you can. How do you read me?"

There was a slight pause, then a man's baritone voice replied, "I read you excellent. No fish in pursuit here. Do you need assistance?"

"How can he sound so calm?" Nestor said.

"Because whoever it is is a professional," Travis said.

Before Jim could respond, the boat lurched forward as something nudged it from behind. Nestor heard someone cry out, then realized it was him.

Travis nodded to his son. "Better let them know we need help. I'm pushing this as fast as I can and if I can't outrun the bastards, we're in a world of trouble."

Swallowing hard, Jim took a moment to compose himself and did his best to express the urgency without sounding as terrified as Nestor was sure he felt. The *SenoRita* shuddered again as another heavy body launched itself against the hull. Nestor was sure he was going to shit himself for the first time since he'd shed his reliance on diapers.

EIGHTEEN

After a long line of expletives, Ken Beekman got himself under control. How in the holy hell was what he was seeing even possible? Those prehistoric-looking fish were demolishing the Coast Guard cutter like it was a paper boat. Everyone on the bridge watched the attack in stunned silence.

Preparing to get the hell away from the overrun cutter, he took the call from the *SenoRita*. He looked to Suzanne and their newest addition. "Any ideas?"

Whit's bronzed skin paled.

"You have any torpedoes aboard?" he said.

"Oh sure," Tom replied. "We keep them with our nuclear-tipped guided missiles. Standard climatologist stuff."

"Tom!" Suzanne snapped.

"Are those fish attracted to movement?" Ken asked. He needed an answer right away. The ship and the lives of everyone on board depended on it.

"No, not standard chimaera fish," Whit said. "But those aren't standard chimaeras."

Bright flashes of light popped like fireflies all over the cutter's deck as everyone aboard came out to repel the aggressive barrage.

Ken started the engine. "No matter. If your friends are in trouble, we can't leave them out there."

"Is there anything aboard we can use as a weapon?" Whit said.

Suzanne looked to be running down a mental checklist. "We have flares and gaffing poles. Oh, and Shirley's gun that may have a few bullets left."

"I take it that we're not talking a big gun?" Whit said.

"She keeps it in her purse."

"Shit." Whit pounded his fist on a table. "You a good shot, Tom?"

"I've been known to hit a bullseye from time to time," Tom said, rising from his seat.

Ken could see the retreating *SenoRita,* along with the dozen or so fish hot on its tail. He'd rather be beating a path away from the fish, but no one deserved what was happening to the Coast Guard, especially a few unarmed men on a party fishing boat. Maybe there was a chance they could scare off the fish and both ships could tear ass back to the mainland.

"Tom, you get the flares and meet me at the bow," Whit said. Tom bolted from the bridge.

"I'm coming with you," Suzanne said.

"Stay in here. I don't want to have to worry about you and try to shoot a target dipping in and out of the water."

"You can't tell me what to do," she said.

"Look, we can replay the greatest hits from our marriage later. Right now, I need you to listen to me. These things won't know how to react to fire. It looks like they hunt in groups. I need to get them to think chasing the *SenoRita* isn't worth the effort...or the pain."

"I can help!"

Ken was gaining on the *SenoRita.*

"There's no time for a goddamn soap opera," Ken barked. "Suzanne, I need you in here. Whit, happy hunting."

The ichthyologist gave him an appreciative nod. Ken had never been divorced, but he knew how ugly things could get. They had enough drama to contend with at the moment. Suzanne was a strong-willed woman, but he knew he'd feel better if his ex-wife was safe while he did the dirty work.

Whit left the bridge, Suzanne running to the window to watch, her hands splayed against the glass.

Tom slapped an orange flare gun in Whit's hand, along with several flares.

"How many flares we got?" Whit asked.

"I scared up two dozen. I set several aside in case we need them later."

He didn't need to explain what they would need them for. It wasn't a stretch to see the *Porpoise IV* ending up in the same straits as the Coast Guard cutter.

The stern of the *SenoRita* was only fifty or so yards away. The chimaera fish were fully intent on capsizing it, smashing it from side to side, bow to stern. The ship juked and jived as if it were caught at the edge of a twister.

"I'd kill to have someone invent a semi-automatic flare gun about now," Whit said. They'd have to shoot them one at a time, precious seconds wasted between ejecting the spent shell and loading the next.

"You know what Mick Jagger said," Tom said. "You can't always get what you want."

Gripping the gun, Whit said, "I thought for sure you were going to say you had some Puerto Rican girls just dying to meet me."

Tom looked at him as if he'd lost all his senses.

Following directly in the *SenoRita's* wake made for a bumpy ride. The nose of the ship canted up, almost taking their feet out from under them.

"This is going to be impossible," Tom said, hooking one leg around the lower rail to support himself. The constant spray of water was already soaking them to their underwear.

Whit did the same. "I like a challenge."

Both taking aim, the first two flares streaked toward the fish trailing the stern. Whit prayed none of the flares would hit the *SenoRita*. Whit's flare fizzled into the ocean. Tom's hit an ascending chimaera right on the top of its head. It quickly dove back down, giving up the chase. Whether it was the flame of the flare or the searing pain when it touched the chimaera's ancient flesh, it was doing the trick.

"And you said it was impossible," Whit said, loading up another. As crazy as it seemed, he was jealous Tom had gotten the first hit. He looked back to see Suzanne staring at them.

This isn't a carnival game to win Suze a teddy bear. All that matters is that we put the fear of fire in those things.

His second shot clipped one near its massive, black eye just before it could veer into the starboard side. Like the one Tom hit, it disappeared back into the ocean. He let out a loud whoop.

Tom's went high and wide, skimming over the top of the *SenoRita*.

"Shit, that was too close," Tom cursed, ramming another shell into the gun.

"This definitely isn't like shooting fish in a barrel," Whit said.

They rested their forearms on the top rail, aimed and fired simultaneously. Both flares hit their marks just as two chimaera leapt like porpoises. Bright sparks sizzled from the back of each fish like tiny volcanoes spewing fireworks. The chimaera spun in the air, crashing dangerously close to the ship. The backwash of water flowed over the ship.

Poor Nestor, Whit thought. *I hope the poor guy hasn't had a heart attack.*

Again and again, they reloaded and pulled their triggers, missing some, but lucking into direct hits. The only reason they were that lucky was because of the sheer number of chimaera fish surrounding the ship.

They only realized their plan was working when their last two shots landed in the water with no fish in sight. And to double their good fortune, the fish hadn't turned on the *Porpoise IV*.

"Holy Havana, I think we did it," Whit said.

Mentioning Havana made him think of frozen daiquiris and mojitos and how much he wanted a drink right now.

"Just in time," Tom said. "Not many more flares left."

"That was pretty good shooting, Sundance," Whit said.

There was no time to congratulate each other. A gargantuan chimaera burst from the water, hovering over the *SenoRita* for a breath-stealing moment before slamming onto the deck with a sickening crunch. The bow of the fishing ship tilted skyward like the end of a teeter-totter.

Whit's mouth went dry. "Oh no. Dear God, no!"

NINETEEN

When Travis saw the first flares, he thought the Coast Guard was shooting at them, maybe for deserting a ship in distress. Crazy idea, but it was the first thing that popped into his overly taxed brain. It was Jim who told him two men were shooting at the devilish fish from the *Porpoise IV*.

Trying to keep the wheel steady was taking every ounce of strength he had. His arms burned liked they were on fire. His fingers curled around the wheel until it felt like his knuckles would pop.

"Jimmy, I want you to strap yourself in," he shouted. "You too, Nestor."

With all of the thrashing the boat was absorbing, he expected to take on serious damage any second. Thoughts of what this foray into madness would cost were as far from his conscious as the stars from the ocean. All that mattered now was surviving.

If their only hope was the Roman candle lightshow going on around them, shit was about as bad as it could get.

He didn't notice the cessation of fish ramming the boat. His fixation was on keeping the *SenoRita* together, going as fast as she could maintain, calculating how incredibly long it would be before he saw land.

And then his worst nightmare came to life.

He heard the stern give way as one of the fish crashed down. One second he was looking at the ocean ahead of them, the next all he could see were stars.

Jim and Nestor cried out. Travis's feet went out from under him, but he kept his handhold on the wheel.

He thought he heard Nestor wail, "We're going to die!"

Not if I can help it.

All that mattered was getting Jim to safety. The *Porpoise IV* was close. They had to abandon ship.

The *SenoRita* settled back down, but the damage was done. The engine sputtered. He could feel her taking on water.

"Life jackets!" he shouted. Jim grabbed three from under his seat, handing them out. He quickly got his on, helping Nestor. The older man's eyes rolled in his head.

Travis grabbed Nestor by his jacket. "We have to get out of here. You understand?"

Nestor nodded, a bubble of snot popping from one of his nostrils.

"Jim, hold on to me," Travis said.

"I got you, Dad." Jim was scared but he still had his wits about him. Travis's chest burned with pride. He'd raised one hell of a kid.

No, Jim was a man.

Emerging from the pilothouse, they stopped at the sight of the giant chimaera fish, its great mouth opening and closing as if it were gasping for air...or in this case, searching for someone to crush. Its oily, dark, mottled body took up the entire stern. Water churned around it.

"There!" Travis pointed.

The *Porpoise IV* was pulling up alongside them. Several people were at the bow's rail holding life preservers attached to thick rope.

Getting in the water to grab a preserver was going to be risky. God only knew how many of those cursed fish were just below the surface, waiting for an easy morsel.

Nestor must have been thinking the same thing, because he said, "I'm not getting in that water."

"You don't have a choice," Travis said. "You stay here long enough and you'll be in the water anyway."

The fish flopped forward, tipping the boat back. All three of them slid closer to the edge of the pilothouse deck. If they flipped over the small rail, it would be there waiting for them.

Spotting Whit's scuba gear, Nestor picked it up and threw it at the fish. It hit the creature right between the eyes. The damn thing didn't even react.

"I hope Whit didn't need that," Nestor said.

"Not unless he's insane," Travis said.

"Hey, we could catch the life preservers in midair and get them to pull us aboard before we hit the water. They'll have to pick up the slack fast and we'll have to jump like Jordan, though," Jim said.

The deck of the *Porpoise IV* was slightly higher than the *SenoRita*. There was no guarantee they wouldn't hit water first, but it was their only option.

"I was never very good at basketball," Nestor said, his face waxen, eyes bulging from his skull.

Travis patted his son's back. "Good thinking. Any way to stay out of the drink."

No sooner had he said it than the first preserver was cast their way. He saw Whit at the other end of the line. It sailed just past their fingertips, dropping into the water.

"Keep trying," Travis shouted up at Whit. "Don't let us go in the water."

Another preserver zipped down. Travis jumped, caught it, then fell. He slid down the deck, slipping under the rail.

"I got you!" Jim screamed, both hands on the shoulders of the life vest. Travis's legs dangled in empty space. If Jim hadn't stopped his slide, he'd be in the chimaera's mouth right now.

"Sorry to disappoint you, you ugly fucker," Travis said to the unfeeling fish, hocking a wad of spit that landed on its lip.

Jim and Nestor pulled him to his feet. Travis handed the preserver to his son. "Go!"

Jim looked reluctant to leave his father.

There were so many things he wanted to say, too many things that should have been said over the years. Travis wasn't an emotional man. He wasn't about to go soft on his son now. He loved him, and Jim damn well knew it.

The *SenoRita* took on water, the deck of the *Porpoise IV* rising further and further away.

Jim clutched the preserver, hooking a leg through it, and was pulled away from the deck. He skimmed dangerously close to the fish, missing it by inches before banging into the *Porpoise IV's* hull. Travis finally took a breath when he saw his son had maintained his hold and was being pulled up.

"Here comes another," he said, grabbing a preserver and handing it to Nestor.

"Thank you," Nestor said.

"Now you really have something to tell your grandkids."

"And so will you."

Travis snagged the next preserver, watching Nestor go through the same motion as his son. Nestor clung to the rope with his eyes closed.

As Travis was putting his leg through his preserver, he heard Jim wail in agony. A chimaera fish, smaller than some of the others but still at least ten feet long, had risen up and latched onto his foot. The men up top couldn't support the sudden additional weight.

Jim cried as he dipped lower and lower, the fish crushing his foot and ankle, the cold ocean getting closer by the second.

"No!"

Travis stepped out of the preserver, tucking it under his arm. Jumping to the lower deck, he twisted his body to avoid the big chimaera's wide-open trap. He grabbed a gaffing pole and leapt, landing on the fish's head. It was too slippery and he thumped on his back.

The line went taught as the people aboard the *Porpoise IV* pulled. Regaining his footing, Travis ran down the fish, aiming for his son and the creature he'd make damned sure would come away empty handed.

TWENTY

Whit couldn't believe what he was seeing. Tom, Raymond and Shirley struggled to keep Jim from being dragged to his death by the chimaera fish. He desperately wanted to help, but he was having a hard enough time getting Nestor up with Suzanne's assistance.

Travis launched himself at the fish wrapped around his son's lower leg. He held the gaffing pole out like a spear, loosening a cry that would have given a Marine pause.

"Keep him even with that fish," Whit shouted at Simon. Veins bulged out of the side of his neck as he did his best to hold onto the swinging captain.

Travis's momentum drove the pole deep into the fish's head. Its mouth opened, and Jim was free. The trio tugged with renewed vigor. The wounded boy was silent, having passed out.

The chimaera disappeared. Whit saw Travis shouting something but couldn't hear the words.

"Come on, let's get them all up pronto!" Tom shouted. With a lot of grunting, Jim and Nestor made it aboard first. Shirley cradled Jim as he lay on the deck. Nestor was on his hands and knees, trying to catch his breath.

Whit rushed to help Simon. He looked down and saw the triumph in Travis's face.

"That was one hell of a move," Whit said.

"No fucking fish is going to take my son from me."

Simon groaned as they pulled Travis up another foot.

"Look out!" Suzanne yelled.

Whit didn't know where to look. Calling on reserves of strength, he pulled as hard as he could.

He and Simon stumbled backwards, falling hard. Whit's head thumped against the deck.

The rope was completely slack. Suzanne's trembling hands fluttered over her mouth.

"It took him," she said. "It took him. I don't even think he saw it. It jumped up and then he was gone."

Dropping the rope, Whit ran to the rail and looked down.

Travis was nowhere to be seen.

"It was so big," Suzanne said. "It swallowed him whole."

Whit's vision reeled, whether from the blow to his head or the cold certainty that Travis was gone. Probably both. He'd yet to see what state Jim's leg was in.

"We can't stay here," Whit said, helping Simon up and grabbing Suzanne by the elbow. "It's not safe. Come on."

They followed everyone making their way to the bridge.

"You care to tell me where it *is* safe?" Simon asked, shoulders slumped, rubbing his sore hands.

Whit wished to hell he had an answer.

Whit watched Tom apply a tourniquet to Jim Hewitt's leg. He was still unconscious in a spare bunk below deck. The poor kid's ankle and foot were crushed beyond repair. It would have to be amputated when they got him to a hospital.

If they got him to a hospital.

Having gotten their literal pound of flesh, the chimaera fish had disappeared. Whit went topside and watched from the rear deck as the *SenoRita* sank, fading to black.

Ken Beekman kept them on a steady course for Miami. Whit and Tom had the flare guns tucked in their belts, all of the spare flare in their pockets. He hoped to God they wouldn't need to use them.

Word of what had happened to them and the Coast Guard spread like wildfire. The Navy was on alert, scuttling ships to be on the lookout for more of the savage sea creatures.

He felt a hand on his shoulder. "I feel so bad, it hurts."

Nestor stood beside him, looking far older than the man who'd first picked him up from the hotel.

"We couldn't have known it would be like this," Whit said. "You can't take all of this on."

Nestor wiped his right eye with the back of his hand.

"Logically, I know that. But nothing that happened tonight is logical."

There was nothing for Whit to say. He could tell him he'd find out how this happened and how to stop them, but that was a tall promise to make. It was one he wasn't sure he'd be able to keep.

There was a chance they could get their bearings once they got on land and had time to think. The answer had to be in the blood and tissues. The big question was, would they find those answers before someone else died?

These aren't questions I ever thought I'd be asking, Whit thought.

He left Nestor staring at the open sea. Suzanne waited for him by the bridge's door. Their eyes met, hers glazed the way they would when she had a fever. He was sure his own were bloodshot and sagging.

"I'm so glad you're here," she said.

She opened her arms and held him. Her body shivered against his. Whit held her tight, wondering what was next. He knew damn sure they were far from safe.

TWENTY-ONE

Robin Raisor, aka The Flash Master, knew he should be enjoying himself. Here he was on a yacht filled with a dozen college girls, drunk off every fruity drink known to man and a baleful of weed, tops flying off for his cameras left and right. Nights like this were every man's dream, right?

Except the constant caterwauling of the drunk coeds had given him a humdinger of a headache.

The next chick who screams Flash Master dot com *in my ear is going overboard!*

The pounding beat of house music from hell didn't make things any better.

Over the past decade and a half, he'd seen so many tits, they no longer…titillated him. Boobs had become clinical objects. When he started his business, selling DVDs of girls flashing their cans for his store-bought camera, he was young and horny and fresh from losing his virginity. Now, he'd trade all of this for a quiet night at home with his girlfriend, Carla, watching classic movies and going to bed early, a warm, loving body pressed beside him.

If he didn't retire this shit soon, Carla wasn't going to be there much longer. He promised her his rep as a world class pussy hound was dead and buried, but he knew it was hard for her to imagine that when he was in a place like this surrounded by nubile, naked girls.

"This night can't end soon enough," he said with a long sigh.

"What's that?" Happy, his assistant director and primary cameraman, asked.

Robin slowly shook his head, pointing at two girls making out by the bar. "Nothing. You getting that?"

"Do you even need to ask?"

Happy was right. His crew had been with him long enough now that they could do this in their sleep.

"Any idea where our host is?" Robin asked.

"I think I saw him slip down to his master cabin with the girl with two-toned hair."

Robin looked around at the partying girls and his crew milling about them. Most of them had two-toned hair. "Which one?"

"Blue and yellow."

Of course. She was the best looking of the lot. It was the price to pay for borrowing the yacht, a gold, two-hundred fifty foot Palmer Johnson Yacht that was shaped slick as a cat's grin. Its owner, some guy from Oklahoma who'd won the Powerball lottery a couple of years back, was only too happy to lend it to them, as long as he got to party with the girls.

"We need to get this to the shower," Robin said. His videos always ended with a XX rated lesbian scene in the shower. The question was, which of the girls here was game?

Happy called a stunning redhead with silicone breasts and a palm tree tattoo on her left hip over.

"Who do you think?" Robin asked her.

The redhead was actually a porn star that went by the name Aurora Canyons. Her real name was something like Lisa Schindler. He couldn't remember. Aurora was his ringer, the girl who got things started. She had an eagle eye for which girls wanted to experiment and take things to the next level.

"Those two," she said, nodding to a pair of brunettes with pink streaks in their hair sitting on the cream-colored leather couch.

"Okay then, do your thing," Robin said.

"I want a grand extra."

She crossed her arms over her massive, inflated chest.

"I already gave you three. And you're not even on camera! I'd like to see you make that after a day of taking it in the ass out in Tampa."

His outburst didn't faze her in the least. "I heard you're thinking of quitting."

"Who told you that?"

She looked at Happy. He was too busy filming to notice.

I'll deal with you later, Robin thought, boring a hole through the top of Happy's head with his irritated gaze.

"So you want to shake me down before I pull the plug, is that right?"

Aurora smiled. "Exactly."

What could he do? She had him in a tight spot.

"Fine. Use it to put your kid through Hebrew school or something."

She flipped him the bird and sauntered over to the girls, the cheeks of her ass jiggling. It only took a minute for her to take both girls by the hand. But instead of taking them down below, she led them to the outside deck.

"What the hell is she doing?" he said to Happy.

"Maybe she realizes one of them needs some air. We don't want them passing out or puking."

Puking might not be so bad. There was a market out there for that. As sleazy as the public thought he was, though, he'd never stoop that low. It was bad enough he was reviled as a pig who took advantage of innocent girls who'd had too much to drink.

Innocent. Right.

They followed the trio outside. Aurora already had one girl in a lip-lock, pulling the other close to her so their breasts touched. They were in a spit swapping triple kiss seconds later. It was too bad he couldn't use this footage. Aurora was contracted for another studio. On his shoots, she was the fluffer.

He and Happy knew to stay silent. They didn't want to break the mood.

Just get them to the shower before my head explodes, he silently pleaded.

The two girls being drunk and on the ocean, started to lose their balance. Without breaking their embrace on one another, all three stumbled to the railing. Robin's heart stopped beating. For a moment, he thought they were going to sail overboard.

"Almost a snuff film there," Happy joked. Robin rapped the back of his head.

"Not funny," Robin whispered.

The girls remained pressed against the rail, hands exploring each other.

At least the air out here was fresh. Robin's headache started slipping away.

"Come on, Aurora, let's get them back inside," he said so low, even Happy couldn't hear.

It looked like she was about to make her move when the sound of a tremendous explosion of water stopped her. The lights on the yacht's deck and Happy's camera caught an enormous, terrifying fish as it leapt into the air, its jaws clamping shut on one of the girls. She was pulled over and out of sight in a split-second.

"Holy shit!" Happy exclaimed, dropping his camera.

Something thundered against the hull of the yacht. The deck vibrated beneath their feet.

"Get away from there!" Robin shouted at the girls. He heard the others shrieking as they ran outside to see what had happened.

Aurora and the remaining girl were locked in place, too terrified to move. He could hear and see other fish. Were they fish or some kind of diseased whale or shark, flipping out of the water, banging their heads against the ship?

I've got to get them out of there!

Looking around, he grabbed a standing champagne bucket and ran to Aurora. Just as he got to her, another fish made it high enough to claim a prize.

Robin stared into its cold, dead eye, its mouth opening, the vile stench of the sea and rotted guts emanating from its maw. He rammed the bucket into its eye with one arm while sweeping the girls away with the other. They hit the deck hard, but they were safe.

For the moment.

The fish jerked hard to the right and slipped out of sight. There was complete pandemonium. Everyone was shouting. The boat felt like it was going to bust apart.

This is a hell of a way to retire, he thought.

Stepping away from the rail, he was stunned to see four of the fish, each of them well over ten feet long, leap onto the deck, scattering chairs and couches, smashing the table they'd had dinner on earlier that night.

The girls panicked, hitting into one another and falling, easily slipping into the fish's eager mouths. When they slammed shut, it was like popping blood-filled balloons.

"No! No! No!" Robin wailed.

If his soul was damned for his past sins, this made him doubly damned. He spied a steak knife on the floor. Happy tried to grab his shirt but he pulled away. "We have to get inside!" Happy shouted.

Fuck that.

If they were going to die here, he was going out with as much good karma as possible. Robin spat a strangled cry and ran to the nearest fish, slicing its upper lip clean in half. He spun and jabbed the one beside it in the gills.

More made their way onto the yacht.

Jesus, can these things fucking fly?

Robin hacked and slashed, unsure if he was doing any real damage to the beasts from the deep.

He was rammed in the back, knocking all the wind from him. The knife clattered to the deck.

Sliding as the yacht canted, he ended up in the middle of several of the demon fish.

Please forgive me.

Something that felt like a stinger pierced his lower leg. Fire erupted in his muscles, traveling up his leg. Whatever poison was in that stinger felt like the flames of hell.

He turned to see another fish chomp down on his arm. It was mashed to a bloody pulp. The pain was horrid, but he didn't black out.

Robin stayed conscious, pain within and without, until his head rolled into an open mouth. Death was a mercy.

TWENTY-TWO

"Dammit!" Ken Beekman hollered.

Whit and Suzanne had been close to dozing off. Tom and everyone else were in their quarters. All aboard were worried about Jim Hewitt. He'd spiked a fever and wasn't looking well at all.

"What's wrong?" Suzanne said, instantly awake.

"We scared those fish off all right, but they're ahead of us now. I just caught a distress signal from a yacht not far from here."

"We can try to go around them," she said. Whit bolted to the forward window, scanning the black ocean waters.

"If only I knew how far that would have to be," Ken said. "Maybe I should stop now, wait for the light of day when we can at least see them coming. Or at the very least I'm going to slow down, try to get a sense for where they're moving."

Whit said, "We certainly don't have the firepower to stop them a second time. Unless."

"Unless what?" Suzanne asked.

Whit sucked on his bottom lip. It was his classic deep thought tic. He usually employed it when he had to decide which microbrew to order when they were out.

He turned to Ken. "You have spare tanks of fuel?"

"You're not setting fire to my ship," Ken warned.

Whit shook him off. "No, but we can light up the water if we need to. Suzanne, can you show me where it would be?"

"Whit, what you're suggesting could get us killed," she said.

"I only plan to use it if it looks like we're riding out the end of our luck, bad as it's been. It's that or pray for divine intervention."

Her blood boiled. How dare he mock her faith at a time like this? It had been his go-to when he wanted to set her over the edge. When she announced their divorce to her parents, her mother gave her an *I told you so* shrug, followed by, "I warned you, Catholics and atheists don't mix."

This from a woman who hadn't seen the inside of a church for close to three decades.

"Really, Whit? You're going there now?"

"I'm sorry, I didn't mean it that way. If they come back at us, though, it's all we've got."

As much as she wanted to fight it, he was right. She hated when he was right.

"Follow me," she said, running to the engine room.

"This is the best you can come up with?" she said, pointing out the red fuel drum. "Set them on fire? I thought you knew these things inside and out."

"I know a ton about chimaera fish, but not *these* chimaera fish. Fire always worked against Frankenstein's monster. It'll work here."

They lugged the heavy drum to the deck, petrol sloshing inside. Whit's face was beet red from exertion, as he took on most of the load. She worried about the hernia he'd had repaired eight years ago.

"They kind of look like the monster," she said.

"Hence my deduction that fire bad."

Amazing. Even in the heart of the deadliest night they had ever experienced, he still managed to be flippant. She used to wish she could let loose like that, pull the stick from her own ass. But one of them had to be the adult.

He asked, "Are there any more methane vents between here and the mainland? It doesn't matter how small."

She didn't need to ask why. More vents meant the possibility of more of those chimaeras. "I don't think so but let me check."

They huddled by her laptop, Whit's chin practically on her shoulder. She could smell the dried sea salt in his unkempt hair. Suzanne opened the file for an oceanographic map where she had plotted all the known release points of methane. Each hot zone was marked by a red dot, the size of the dot larger or smaller depending on the methane amounts measured. She found their current location atop the methane vent, her finger tracing a route all the way to Miami.

"We should be clear, but you can see right there, we have one off of Key West and another up there a few miles from Boca Raton."

"Are three that close together normal?"

"Now it is. Ten years ago, it would have set off alarm bells."

Whit drew an imaginary line between the three red dots. "A triangle intersecting with the Bermuda Triangle. The kid in me who loved all those mystery shows would have traded anything to be here. As it stands, the adult in me would trade anything to get the hell home – with several of those chimaera fish in captivity, of course. I could spend two lifetimes studying those bastards."

He looked beat to hell. The swollen bellows under his eyes had sprouted a second set of bags. Suzanne was sure she didn't look much better.

She said, "Let's just hope those other two locations are too small to be of any significance."

Checking his watch, Whit said, "Couple of hours until daylight. I'm tempted to call Garret about the results of the toxin samples I sent out, but I know there won't be anything yet. I'll stress the urgency first thing in the morning."

They sat in silence, staring at her laptop's screen.

So many red dots, especially in the Pacific and near the North Pole. If the public only knew how close they were to calamity.

"Maybe it won't end with fire and ice, but with the past coming up to consume our future," she said.

Whit raised an eyebrow.

"I keep thinking about that Coast Guard cutter. The way those chimaeras swarmed it. Do you think they could have made it out?"

He put an arm around her. It felt familiar, comfortable and strange, all at the same time. "Ken says he hasn't heard from them in a while. We should expect the worst. Come on, why don't you get some sleep? I'll keep old Ken awake."

She rose from her chair, his arm slipping away. "No, this is my ship. I can sleep later."

Getting Ken a fresh cup of coffee, she prayed that the chimaeras in their path had moved off to deeper waters where there were fewer civilians to terrorize.

TWENTY-THREE

A harsh shaft of sunlight woke Shirley from a deep, deep sleep. Squinting at the porthole, she shook off the cobwebs as fast as she could. She wanted to check the poor kid in the next room.

She'd slept in her clothes and Doc Martens, prepared to make a run for it if needed. The kid, Jim, was asleep. She placed a hand on his forehead, felt the clammy heat on her palm. He was on fire. Her hand came away slick with sweat. Running a washcloth under cold water, she wiped his face and head, slicking his hair back.

Jim didn't move. His eyelids didn't even so much as flutter.

He wasn't just sleeping. He was unconscious, maybe even in a coma. But what did she know? She was no doctor.

The dressing on his pulverized leg was soaked through with blood. It pooled on the sheet under his leg.

"I'll have to change that," she said.

Tom popped his head in, startling her. "How's he doing?"

"Not good. I want to take his temperature and change his bandages."

"Anything I can do to help?"

"Actually, yeah. You think you can gently lift his leg up while I unwrap the bandage?"

He eagerly came into the room. That was Tom. They called him the Good Samaritan behind his back. If he knew they held him in such high esteem, it might go to his head. Best to say it when he wasn't around to hear it.

"Okay, you take the lower half and I'll take the upper so I can find where the bandage ends," she said.

The smell coming off his leg was bad. Infected kind of bad. Shirley had to breathe through her mouth, which only made her taste it.

"That's not good at all," Tom said, angling himself so he could slip his hand under the boy's calf.

"I'm almost afraid to look," Shirley said, pausing a moment before taking hold of his thigh.

As soon as she touched his leg, she knew something was wrong. Tom hissed.

"Hold up, hold up," he said.

But it was too late. Jim's leg had turned to the consistency of tapioca. The flesh and bone squished between their fingers. Shirley yelped, dropping his leg onto the bed.

Jim started convulsing.

Tom took out his wallet and tried to jam it in Jim's mouth, but it was closed tight as a bank vault. White froth bubbled from his nostrils.

Shirley's hands were covered in blood. She held the boy down by the shoulders. Tom did the same with his torso.

Jim's mouth gaped open, the ragged sound of his drawing breath monstrous to hear. His stomach expanded, then collapsed. He went still. Shirley watched in horror as his bandaged leg deflated, viscera seeping through the gauze.

"Get Whit and Suzanne down here now!" Shirley screamed.

"Right. Right." Tom looked dazed.

The moment he left the room, Shirley ran to the sink to wash her hands.

Holy shit. If whatever he had is contagious, we're screwed!

She was drying off her hands when the boat rocked, knocking her off her feet. Jim slipped off the bed, landing with a wet splat. Shirley screamed, scrambling to get out of the room. The stench alone was enough to send her senses reeling.

Once in the hallway, Raymond almost trampled over her.

"Did you feel that?" he said, the whites of his eyes bulging.

"How could I not? Help me up."

When he went to grab her hand, she pulled away. If she was infected, she didn't want to pass it along to him. "Never mind, I'll manage."

She followed him to the bridge. Everyone was there, staring out the bow window. The first thing she saw was the normal scattering of fishing boats, a few sailboats thrown in the mix.

But that wasn't what had everyone's attention.

"Oh my God," she said, staggering into the wall.

The safety of Miami's shore was just visible. They were so close.

But to get there, they'd have to run a gauntlet of prehistoric fish gone mad.

"We can't catch a damn break," Ken spat, keeping the wheel steady as an unseen chimaera fish whammed into the *Porpoise IV*'s hull.

Suzanne shouted, "Where the hell is the Navy?"

The scene before them was something out of a drug-induced nightmare, a heroin overdose in an abandoned house where the veil between life and death was thin as gossamer.

Chimaera fish, their tan, blotchy flesh glinting with sunlight as they shot from the deep, were everywhere. There wasn't a single boat on the water that was spared. Masts swayed and shuddered as some ships took on water. The decks of others listed as they were weighted down by the ravenous creatures.

Whit was sure that if they cut the engine, the air would be filled with the terrified shrieks of hundreds of people facing a death too alien to comprehend.

"The Navy is probably out where that cutter and the *SenoRita* went down, looking for more of them," Whit said. *Which means we're on our own.*

If these chimaeras were indeed resurrected from a time older than they thought possible, they must have been the dominant species in the forming oceans. A predator with no equal. Anything and everything around them was fair game. The ships and people out here were nothing but high-end feeder fish.

And now the chimaeras knew the *Porpoise IV* was in their midst. The radio crackled with the frantic cries of mayday.

Ken looked to him. "Any ideas?"

Heading back to sea seemed safe, but it just put them further from where they needed to be. They could try to circumnavigate the chaos. Something told him a contingent of the chimaeras would simply follow.

Which left attempting to plow through the feeding frenzy.

"I have a few, and all of them are pretty bad," Whit said. There was a sharp barrage of chimaera bodies against the hull. They wanted inside bad. "We're just going to have to try to get as close to shore as possible."

Tom looked at him as if he'd lost his mind. Whit saw that there was a considerable amount of blood on his hands. What the hell? "Anything less than the shore is death."

The *Porpoise IV* shivered.

"We don't have any choice," Suzanne said.

Nestor was staying unusually quiet, his lips moving frantically. Whit realized he was praying. He sidled next to Nestor. "We're going to get out of this. Somehow, someway."

"From your lips to God's ears," he replied, eyes moving heavenward. "This is maybe a little more adventure than I bargained for."

Whit squeezed his shoulder. "You and me both, buddy."

"I say we get the hell out of here and make our way to South Damn Africa if we need to," Simon barked. "This coast is fucked. There are other places to go, you know."

Ken's shoulders stiffened. "We'll never make it," he said. "She's taking too much damage. Those things are like a dog with a bone. They won't stop until we're sunk."

Simon spewed a string of indecipherable curses, his hands balled into fists. Whit shot Tom a look that said *if he makes a move toward Ken, we take him down.*

To his relief, Simon sagged once he vented his intense displeasure.

Whit said to him, "Don't count us out yet. We may have a way to keep them at bay. If the other ships see it, maybe a few of them could follow suit."

Simon shook his head. "You find more flares? There's not enough in a freaking flare factory to chase them off."

"Even better. I found a whole emergency kit with handheld flares. Why don't you, me and Tom head outside and I'll show you. And grab those flares over there. Ken, the key is to stay on course and don't slow down. Give the horn a blast when you think it's getting to be too much."

Ken looked at him quizzically.

"Just trust me."

"Like I have any other choice," Ken said, tightening his grip on the wheel.

Simon followed Tom out the door. Before Whit could leave, Suzanne grabbed his arm. "Please be careful."

"I think we passed careful about twelve hours ago. Nestor, watch my lovely ex and make sure she doesn't do anything stupid like follow me outside, okay?"

"This is her ship. Why would she listen to me?" he said, hat in his hands, crushing the narrow brim.

"He's right, you know," Suzanne said.

"Promise me, you'll stay in here," Whit said.

She caressed his cheek. "I promise. The brawn has to protect the brains, you know."

He wanted to kiss her, to feel her lips again, something he never knew how much he'd missed until now. Instead, he turned to Raymond and said, "Come on, I need your help, too."

Raymond's shoulders sagged. "Of course you do."

Whit clapped him on the shoulder. The climatologist nearly fell forward.

They staggered as the ship swayed under the chimaeras' assault.

Whit said to Tom, "What happened to your hands?"

Tom's face paled. "It's Jim's blood. I'll tell you later. If there is a later."

Whit pointed to the fuel drum. It must have held 20 gallons of petrol. He wished it were more. Hours earlier, he'd found something to pry the lid open as well as empty plastic water jugs to scoop the fuel out.

"I know our parents warned us not to play with fire," Whit said, "but we're going to have to throw convention out the window. For now, just hold on tight. The moment Ken hits that horn, fill up those water jugs and toss the fuel on the water around the ship. We'll light the chimaeras up before they can take us down. With any luck, it'll scare them off."

Simon grabbed him by the collar. "You want us to set the ocean on fire?"

"Just a very small part of it."

Tom shouted, "Jesus, look!"

Whatever boats not already sinking were on the cusp of going down. It was like a scene out of a World War II movie, only the kamikazes in this case were the overgrown chimaeras. The ocean's surface was a mix of red and black as oil oozed from the broken ships.

"We're going to have to just plow right through," Whit said, loosening Simon's hands from his shirt.

"The *Porpoise IV* isn't a damn icebreaker," Simon said, his gaze locked on the carnage.

"We'll have to pretend she is one for now," Whit said. He hoped to hell they wouldn't have to resort to his plan, but getting to shore looked more doubtful by the second. Maybe they should have headed for another coast. No, Ken was right. They'd never make it. This was the only way, as awful as it seemed.

A sailboat fell to its side, the two occupants swallowed up by chimaera fish the moment they leapt off the deck. A fountain of blood spewed from one of the beast's mouth before it descended with its meal.

They passed by a party fishing boat on their left. This close, they could hear the desperate screams of the men aboard. Several chimaeras had made it on board. Whit watched in mute horror as men scrambling to get away fell onto the great fish's heads, pricked by the poisonous stingers hidden next to their front dorsal fins, instantly immobilized and screeching until their vocal chords gave way.

"I don't know how much more she can take," Tom said, gripping a handrail for dear life. Raymond hadn't spoken a word, his eyes so wide Whit thought they might roll from their sockets.

"Ladies have far more pain tolerance than men," Whit said.

A resounding crack sent an icy shiver down his spine.

"The hull must have been breached," Simon wailed, looking to Whit as if he were responsible.

Before he could respond, the ship's horn blared. The *Porpoise IV* began to lose speed.

"Time to play with fire!" Whit said.

Land was in sight, but if they were taking on serious water, they'd never make it.

It's better to try than sit around like a floating appetizer platter, Whit thought, flipping the lid off the container and dipping the water jug inside.

Three other containers jammed in beside his. "Be careful not to —"

Raymond and Tom were dashing to the other side of the ship before he could finish.

"Get any on you," he said. Simon wasn't listening either. He took his jug to the bow.

The ship went slower and slower, listing to the starboard side. A chimaera broke the surface, smashing its head against the guardrail by Whit. He staggered as far away as he could.

He'd spent a decade around these fish, living harmoniously with deep sea creatures that looked straight from a madman's nightmares. The discordance between everything he'd dedicated his life to and the pandemonium they faced made his head spin.

From his vantage point, he could see Simon and Raymond. Tom was on the other side of the ship.

"Wait until we stop!" he warned them.

The *Porpoise IV* crept along, surrounded by the dying cries of mostly men, boats large and small being claimed by the sea. It was an out and out slaughter.

He glanced at Suzanne through the window. He'd never seen her look so scared. He was sure she was thinking the same thing about him. Giving the best faltering smile he could muster, he turned back to the ocean, wary of any chimaeras darting in the air.

With land still too far for the odds of making it back alive to be in their favor, the *Porpoise IV*'s engines gave one last gasp and died.

This is it!

"Now! Now! Now!" Whit shouted.

The four men scattered the fuel atop the choppy ocean that was boiling with writhing chimaera bodies.

Whit grabbed the flare from his pocket, struck the tip to life and tossed it overboard.

The water lit up with a great *whoosh!* Chimaeras nudging the surface dove for cover.

Simon did the same, whooping with delight when one of the fish that had been splashed with fuel torched up like an amphibian Ghost Rider.

Raymond screamed.

Whit turned and felt his heart sink to his shoes.

The man was on fire, stumbling around the stern. Black smoke billowed from the top of his head.

Whit and Simon ran to him, Tom joining from the other side, holding a blue tarp. He threw it over Raymond to douse the flames, tackling him in the process.

"He must have gotten fuel on him," Simon said, helping Tom pat the tarp down around Raymond. The scientist had fallen silent.

"I think it's out," Whit said, pulling at one end of the tarp.

When they revealed Raymond's body, Whit's knees buckled.

TWENTY-FOUR

Raymond Basu was a blackened mess. His clothes had melded with his charred flesh. All of his hair was gone, as well as his lips and eyelids. His eyes stared at them, past them, to a place where every second was an agony.

Whit's stomach roiled at the barbecued pork smell coming off the man.

Worse still, Raymond was alive, his chest rising in ragged gasps.

"Good Christ," Simon muttered, turning away.

Tom looked stricken.

He knew there was no saving the man. Raymond's breath was both raspy and gurgling as his lungs filled with fluid.

The chimaera fish were relentless, ramming the stern. "Simon, you have the extra flares. You need to chuck one over."

Simon nodded, staying clear of the damaged stern and tossing a flare in a looping arc. Whit heard the fuel ignite. That should buy them some time.

"Ray, can you hear me?" Tom said, close to what remained of his colleague's ear.

His eye moved slightly in Tom's direction, but that was all he could do.

Please don't tell me he's conscious! Whit thought. The only mercy would be for his heart to stop.

"We have to get him inside," Tom said.

"There's no point. We're sinking," Whit said. For a moment, he thought Tom was going to punch him.

"Those fucking things are scattering," Simon said. "But what the hell do we do when the ship goes down? The flames will make quick work of our life rafts."

Whit wanted to shout at the man. How the hell did he know what they needed to do? Why couldn't someone else come up with a plan? Because he was the chimaera fish expert, he was also supposed to be the survival professional?

Just calm down, Whit. Calm down and think.

Tom held Raymond's hand. Bits of the man's flesh flaked off under Tom's gentle grasp.

Raymond suddenly went stiff, his eyes rolling. His mouth opened wide, pulling in a great lungful of air.

In the next instant, he was still.

Eyes shimmering, Tom placed his hand by his side.

"He and his wife just had their first child three months ago," Tom said, rising.

Simon was adding more fuel to the water as the *Porpoise IV* listed. He wanted to get as many chimaeras away from them as possible.

Whit said, "We have to get everyone and prepare the life raft."

Tom looked at him as if from a great distance. "I'll get Suzanne, Shirley and Ken."

Whit was about to refill his water jug with more fuel when an enormous chimaera fish broke through the fiery waves, skidding along the stern's deck. It knocked Tom's legs out from under him.

Tom flopped backwards, landing atop the great fish's head. Whit knew in an instant that his back had been pierced by its venomous spine.

Tom screamed in bloody agony.

Running to his aid, Whit jumped to avoid the chimaera's waiting mouth. He slid over its wet body, felt the incredible strength under its ice-cold flesh. Grabbing Tom by the waist, they both rolled to its side. Somehow, he managed to drag Tom away from the flailing fish. It laid waste to everything around it, its massive body splintering wood and warping metal.

The ship tilted backwards by several more degrees, depositing the chimaera back into the flames.

Every muscle in Tom's body was as taut as a drum skin. He looked to be in excruciating pain.

"Holy shit it burns," he managed to croak through clamped teeth. Whit held onto him.

Tom tried to sit upright, using Whit to balance himself.

"How fast will this kill me?" he asked.

Already his eyes were blood red, his skin turning jaundice.

"I…I don't know," Whit said. "I'm not even sure how much venom these things can inject or how it works. Not for something this size."

"Get me the flare gun, then get everyone off the ship."

"No, you're coming with us."

Tom shook his head. "I'll give you some cover. Wish I could clear a path for you all to shore."

Whit knew there was no time to argue with the man. He was right. The venom would kill him, and judging by the chimaera's size and Tom's instant reaction, it wouldn't take long.

He had Suzanne and the rest to think about now.

"Hang tight, okay?"

"I'm about as tight as I've ever been," Tom said, the slight chuckle morphing into a long groan.

Whit grabbed Simon. "Get the life raft ready!"

The man ran to retrieve the inflatable life raft.

Whit opened the bridge door to find Suzanne, Nestor and Shirley standing in the doorway. Ken was on the radio, talking to what sounded like the Coast Guard. They all had life preservers on.

"They have several armed cutters en route," Suzanne said.

"We have to get off the ship now," Whit said.

"I heard screaming," Suzanne said. "What happened?"

He took a breath. "Raymond's gone. Tom got stung. He's hanging on, but it won't be long."

"No!" Suzanne's eyes flooded with tears.

"Stung?" Nestor said. He bit his lower lip.

"We don't have time," Whit said. "Ken, come on!"

The hull of the *Porpoise IV* grumbled as it took on more water.

Ken signed off, ushering everyone outside. Whit told him what had happened. Ken slammed a fist against the door, but said nothing.

Simon had the life raft set to go.

"There's a gap in the flames where we can drop it," he said. "I added several more jugs we can take with us to keep them at bay."

"I'll help you," Shirley said. She, Ken and Nestor went to Simon's side, grappling the raft to get it in the water. A stiff breeze blew Nestor's fedora off his head, depositing it in the ocean.

"They can have the hat as long as they leave us be," he muttered, the cords in his neck bulging as he lowered the raft. "Damn *putas*!"

"I want to see Tom," Suzanne said.

"Come with me," Whit said, grasping her hand.

Tom was where he'd left him. His skin looked like wax, his mouth hanging open. For a moment, he worried that the toxin had already done its dirty work.

When Tom saw Suzanne, he tried to pull himself up straighter, failing.

Dropping to her knees, Suzanne cradled his head against her chest. She couldn't say anything lest she break out in sobs. Whit handed him the flare gun.

"Dump the rest of the fuel on the deck," Tom said through pained gasps. "I'll give them something to think about."

Whit looked into his reddening eyes and nodded. Tom and the *Porpoise IV* had one last surprise left up their sleeves. It was easy to roll the barrel now that the deck was tilted toward the fast sinking stern. He kicked it over, the remaining fuel splashing everywhere.

When he went back to get Suzanne, Tom was grasping her hands.

He said, "You break her heart twice and I'll come back to kick your ass."

"Oh, Tom," Suzanne croaked.

"Both of you, go," Tom said. "Get to shore and find out how to stop these things."

Suzanne said, "No, you have to come with us."

As if to prove why he couldn't, Tom coughed, red and black spittle spattering his chest.

"Go!"

"Come on, Suze," Whit said, reaching down for her. Reluctantly, she got to her feet, eyes never leaving Tom as they walked to the waiting raft. He took one last glance back at Tom. He lifted the flare gun up, letting him know he was ready.

"I won't give you a reason to come back," Whit said softly.

He helped Suzanne into the life raft.

Shirley had her gun in her hand, scouring the water.

Whit got in and they shoved off from the *Porpoise IV*. The heat from the flames was severe enough to make it feel as if his eyelashes were being singed.

They heard the pop of the flare gun. Then another. The visible part of the ship ignited, forming a great barrier of flame at their back. Ken and Simon paddled as hard as they could to distance themselves from the flames and suction of the sinking ship.

"I'm sorry I got you into this," Whit said.

Nestor wiped his hand across his sweaty face. "It was meant to be. We take what we're given."

Whit held his weeping ex-wife.

He wondered how long they had before they rejoined Tom and Raymond.

TWENTY-FIVE

Suzanne couldn't believe her eyes.

Four Coast Guard cutters cleaved their way through the ravenous fish and their wake of destruction, saving as many people as they could. These ships were the biggest in the fleet, and she assumed they were armed to the teeth. One of the cutters made a beeline for their raft.

It wasn't enough. Despite what had happened to one of their own, the Coast Guard had underestimated the threat the chimaera fish posed. She couldn't blame them. Who in the world could anticipate this? It was sheer madness.

Simon was at the ready with their remaining fuel, cursing and daring the chimaeras to make a play for them. Suzanne wished he'd shut the hell up. If just one of those massive fish went for the raft, they were all as good as dead.

Their raft bobbed within a floating ring of flame. It wouldn't be long until the fuel ran out, and then they were in real trouble.

The staccato of automatic fire was a welcome sound as Guardsmen, better prepared than the poor souls who came to their aid just yesterday, fired round after round at the fish the moment they popped up.

"How many can there be, Whit?" she said, staring wide-eyed at the never-ending stream of chimaera fish, some just rising to the surface, others exploding like magma from an angry volcano. With some of the larger ones, she wasn't sure if the bullets had any effect on them.

"A whole hell of a lot more than I'd like," he said. They sat side-by-side, arms and legs touching, feeling each other's tension.

Something large swam just under the raft. They had to hold on as it rocked along the waves. Simon almost dumped all the fuel, holding off when he didn't see any chimaeras appear.

"They're feeling us out," Simon said.

"They're vicious, but I don't think they're that smart," Whit replied. Suzanne detected the hint of doubt in his voice. "Just hold on until we really need it."

And what then, Suzanne thought. *We choose to die by fire rather than being poisoned or crushed by the chimaeras?* How long would they burn, covered in slick fuel, before the waters put them out and they were left at the mercy of the insatiable chimaera?

To her relief, it didn't have to come to that.

The cutter was beside them just as a large chimaera breached the surface, its onyx eye glaring at them before it returned to the deep. Nestor made a nervous hoot, almost flipping over the edge of the raft when he tossed a hand flare at it. Suzanne and Whit grabbed hold of him.

"Just hold it together a little longer, all right buddy?" Whit said.

Nestor nodded, swallowing hard. "I almost had him. At least that's what I'll tell myself later."

"You and Shirley first," Whit said to Suzanne as he grabbed the life preserver that had been tossed down to them. They were pulled aboard so quickly it hurt.

She didn't care if they broke a bone. They knew how fast those fish were and how easily they could leap to get what they wanted. Time was not a commodity they could waste if they wanted to save them.

Nestor came next, then Simon and Whit.

Shirley let out a blood-chilling scream as a chimaera rose just under the raft, knocking Ken overboard. Arms knifing through the water, he swam to the cutter as fast as he could. Water slick and burning with gas lit Ken's arm momentarily before he dove under water. He popped back up, gasping for air.

"I can feel one by my feet!" he exclaimed.

Whit was almost on board, dangling a dozen feet over Ken.

"Get him a preserver!" Whit shouted.

"It's right under me!"

"Just hold on!"

And suddenly, Ken was gone. A preserver hit the water, but there was no one to grab hold. Suzanne screamed his name.

"Do you see him?" she asked Shirley and Simon.

All eyes were on the water, but Ken never reappeared.

She didn't even notice when Whit was standing next to her. He gently took her by the shoulders. "Come on, it's not safe here."

"But...Ken...he could be down there now!"

"He's gone, Suze. There's nothing we can do, except get back in one piece. We're going to have to come up with a way to eradicate them completely. They...they don't belong here."

Suzanne felt numb. She'd lost almost her entire crew, her true family. She wanted to protest, to fight Whit's tug away from the side of the ship, but her legs somehow moved without feeling the ground. One of the Guardsmen draped a beige blanket over their shoulders.

"I need to speak to the ship's captain," Whit said.

A crew cut kid, he couldn't be older than twenty, said, "He's a little busy at the moment."

"I'm one of the few people on the planet who specializes in these fish...or at least the ones that aren't the size of buses and out for blood. I need to make a request. It's very important if we ever hope to stop these things."

The kid weighed his response, eyes furtively looking around at his brothers shooting into the ocean, rescued survivors walking about in a daze.

"How do I know you are who you say you are?"

Suzanne said, "I can vouch for him." She gave her credentials, stressing the government-owned research vessel that they had just abandoned. If he asked ask her for some I.D., she was tempted to tell him he was free to dive in and find it.

Instead, he said, "Come with me."

Suzanne grabbed Shirley's hand. "We'll be back."

"You're leaving me with him?"

Simon looked as if he'd caved in on himself. Whatever piss and vinegar kept the man going day in and day out had been drained away. He looked ready to pass out, the blink of each eye taking longer and longer to complete.

119

"Take good care of him," Suzanne said.

"I'll take care of both of them," Nestor said. He carried three bottles of water. He looked more in control of himself now, the relative safety of the ship probably calming some very frayed nerves. They weren't out of it yet, but they also weren't sinking.

Whit said to him, "You better rest up. Who else is going to drive me all around Miami?"

Nestor gave a half-smile. "As long as we're on land, I'll take you anywhere you want to go. No more oceans for me."

TWENTY-SIX

It took a quick background check before Whit was granted his specific requests. The commander of the cutter, Captain Adams, a fiftyish man with flinty eyes and a nose that looked like it had seen the bad end of many a boxing glove, heard him out. He agreed that with toxin samples from the first fish that was caught already in process, Whit was the person one step ahead of everyone else.

"What you're asking isn't easy," he said with a slight Southern drawl.

"I wouldn't ask if it wasn't necessary. Any way out of this clusterfuck is going to be tougher than shoe leather."

Captain Adams narrowed his gaze at them. "Why don't you two sit tight and let me run the show from here on. I'll get you what you need. You can count on that."

Whit and Suzanne watched the faltering carnage from the safety of the cutter's bridge. With less and less people and boats in the water, the chimaeras were finally beginning to thin out. The men below them were still busy pulling people to safety while dropping as much lead as possible into the Atlantic.

"Do you think he can pull it off?" Suzanne asked.

"I think Captain Adams seems like a guy who does whatever he sets his mind to. Without live fish to test my theories on, we'll just be swinging blindfolded. And if what I'm thinking is right, there may be a way to put an end to them."

Now she turned to him. "And just what are you thinking?"

"I have you to thank for this. You may have been right from the get-go. As improbable as it seems, let's say that yes, these chimaera fish have somehow remained frozen for millions and millions of years, only to be revived thanks to our old pal, Mr.

Global Warming. That means their systems are adapted to an ecosystem that no longer exists. In terms of evolution, they're lagging so far behind everything else in the ocean that they are, despite appearances and actions, behind the proverbial eight ball."

"Proverbial eight ball?"

"I'm tired. It's the best I can come up with. In essence, they're going to die out. The problem is, I don't know how long it will take. And Lord knows how many more lives they'll take before that does happen. We don't have time to sit back and find out."

Suzanne leaned her forehead against the window. She looked ready to collapse. He'd make sure she got straight to bed once they made land. Whereas he still had a hell of a lot ahead of him.

"What makes you so sure they're going to die out?" she said. He thought he saw fresh tears brewing.

"What was my favorite movie when we were dating?"

Closing her eyes, she said, "What does that have to do with any of this?"

He rubbed her back. "Think, Suze. What sci-fi movie did I make you watch over and over again?"

She gave a slight chuckle. "That one with the Martian invasion. Of all the movies, you were addicted to the one where you could even see the strings holding the little models afloat. You and that *War of the Worlds*."

Snapping his fingers, he said, "Exactly! And what killed the Martians? Bacteria. Microscopic organisms that the aliens hadn't evolved with or could adapt to. Those chimaeras might as well be from Jupiter, they're so removed from our world. I just need to find a way to speed their demise along."

"Now you're sounding as crazy as I did."

Whit rubbed his hands over his face. God he'd kill for a drink right about now. A few glasses of very expensive whiskey, a couple of cold beers and a comfortable bed. What he wouldn't give for that.

You can save the booze to celebrate later or drown your sorrows.

He looked at Suzanne, dead on her feet.

Or if there's a chance we could get it right the second time around, whiskey can take a hike.

"Let's go check on Shirley and Simon," Whit said. "There's nothing more we can do until we get back to Miami."

It seemed the entire city, if not half the country, was waiting for the return of the cutters and their grateful occupants. The throng of reporters was almost as terrifying as the hordes of chimaera fish. This was big news, and the world wanted details.

Luckily for them, Captain Adams kept Whit, Suzanne, Nestor, Shirley and Simon out of the spotlight. Several of his men escorted them off the ship and into a waiting Jeep where they were first taken to the hotel where Whit had been registered.

"You both have rooms waiting for you," Whit said to Shirley and Simon. He'd called ahead and made reservations while they were waiting to get off the ship.

Simon opened the door, one foot on the pavement. "What about the rest of you?"

"Got a couple more stops to make. Hey, you did good back there. We wouldn't be here if it weren't for you."

Simon waved him off. "I wouldn't use the word *good* to describe any of this."

Shirley hugged Suzanne and Whit. "I'm going straight to the hotel bar. I'm exhausted but I don't know how I can sleep after all this."

"I think I'll join you," Simon said.

"Call me before you do anything else," Shirley said. "I want to be with you when you find a way to get back at those things. For Danny, you know?"

"I do. And I will," Suzanne said.

The next stop was the marina where Nestor had left his car. Whit stepped outside and walked him to it. There was a ticket on the windshield. Whit grabbed it and stuffed it in his pocket.

"No way you're paying that," he said.

Nestor looked like he was about to argue, raised a finger, lowered it and shook his head.

"You sure you're okay to drive?" Whit asked.

"I'll be fine. My house isn't too far. I can keep my eyes open until then."

"I'm so sorry about everything. Please have Julie May call me in a few days. I want to see what I can do to set things right for Travis's family."

He thought, *was Jim his only son? I'll have to explain everything to his ex-wife.*

It wasn't going to be easy, but he didn't want anyone else to do it. Better it should come from someone who was there, especially the man responsible for her losses.

Nestor grabbed his hand and shook it. "You have nothing to apologize about. No one could have seen this coming."

He was right about that.

"I'll call you when everything is done," Whit said.

"I know you will. And I know you'll find a way to stop them. You have a good woman in there. You work as a team, and I might feel sorry for those chimaeras."

The retired man turned, shoulders a little less square than normal, and slumped into his car. As he sped off, he honked his horn once.

Back in the Jeep, Whit said to Suzanne, "We never did go to an aquarium when we were dating, did we?"

But she was already asleep.

The phrase *Look what the cat dragged in* came to mind when Dhalia Shields saw Whit and the red-headed woman walk into her office. They looked like they should be in a hospital bed getting several IVs, not here.

She rose from her desk. "Oh my God, I've been watching everything on the news. Is Nestor..."

"He's fine," Whit said. "A little worse for wear, but he's most likely home as we speak, passed out on the couch."

Dhalia breathed a sigh of relief. She really liked Nestor. He was like the cool but quiet uncle who slipped you five bucks whenever you came to visit.

"You really should have stopped to get some rest. None of the specimens have arrived yet."

"I want to be here the moment they do. Oh, Dhalia Shields, this is my ex-wife, Suzanne Merriweather."

Suzanne gave her a small finger wave. "I'm sorry, I don't normally look like the walking dead."

"From what I saw, it's a miracle you're even standing. Please, sit down." She ushered them both to the leather loveseat in the corner of her office.

"You mind if I commandeer your phone and computer?" Whit said.

"No. Please, my office is your office. You must be pretty high up for me to get a call from some Coast Guard CO letting me know you're going to need to use the aquarium as a temporary base of operations."

"I've been busy since we last met," he said, settling behind her desk. "I just need to call my colleague to get the toxicology report on the little friend we had here earlier. That could hold the key to everything."

Dahlia settled next to Suzanne. She could see how they would have been married. Both were good looking and obviously smart. Birds of a feather.

"Whit, I attached a zip file with all of the methane vent data and sent it to you, copying myself, while I was on my ship," Suzanne said. The words *my ship* choked off as she said them.

"Perfect," he said, pecking at the keys with four fingers.

"Is there anything I can do?" Dhalia asked.

Suzanne got up from the loveseat with a groan. "Yes. Can you point me in the direction of some hot coffee?"

Her head must have spun, because her eyes rolled for a bit and her arms reached out to steady herself.

Dhalia took her arm. "I'll take you there."

"Thank you."

"Bring a cup back for you?" Dhalia asked Whit.

"Three please. Black, two sugars." His head was buried behind her monitor.

If the fate of the ocean waters was depending on both of them, Dhalia figured she'd have to have a Starbucks kiosk installed right outside the door.

TWENTY-SEVEN

The toxicology report had everyone mystified. The venom from the chimaera fish was unlike anything anyone had ever seen.

As Whit read the report, he couldn't stop smiling. He showed it to Suzanne, who read it with a nail between her teeth. They'd both gotten some sleep the night before, taking turns on Dhalia's loveseat. He was sure they were both pretty ripe by now, but they'd gotten used to it.

Poor Dhalia, he thought.

"So if the venom is that much of an unknown, it'll take years to find an anti-venom," Suzanne said.

"It proves my point that we don't have time to find an anti-venom. Not at this point. When I first sent it to Garrett, I was just curious. How could normally benign venom, at least to humans, take a man's life? The stakes have changed since then," Whit said, tapping a finger on the computer screen. "This just confirms everything. We can't fight off the venom because it's completely alien to us. On the flip side, they won't be able to overcome a modern day virus. From their blood work, we can see that their immune systems are wide open to just about anything in existence today. I already have one in mind and a way to get it down their gullets. We just need to test it and see how it works."

They left Dhalia's office, heading for the alternate whale tank. Overnight, the Coast Guard had delivered two live chimaera fish, one just over ten feet long, the other a shade under eighteen feet. Dead chimaeras weren't going to be a problem to find. Their bullet-riddled, bloated bodies had been washing up on the shore for the past twelve hours. The beaches were cordoned off, filled to capacity with scientists and government officials instead of sunbathers.

The solid steel tank made it impossible to see the chimaeras. Standing along the catwalk above the tank was off limits. Jumping from the water came too easily for them. They were being recorded by a pair of cameras mounted overhead.

Whit rapped his knuckles against the tank. He was answered by a pair of dull thuds.

"What's the plan?" Suzanne asked.

"In a few hours, I'm expecting a delivery of VHS. Not the tape, mind you. The full name is *viral hemorrhagic septicemia*. This stuff is lethal. It's been responsible for several major fish kills over the years. I'm going to inject it in some cut bait and see how long it takes the chimaeras to basically bleed to death internally. They used to house the virus at the Plum Island facility in New York. Remember that vacation we took in Montauk? That and a host of other deadly diseases were just a mile or so away from our spot on the beach. I just found out everything's been moved to Kansas now. I've been out of the country too long."

Suzanne visibly shivered. "And to think that was probably the best time we ever had on vacation. I've heard of VHS, even saw some pictures of a fish kill in one of the lakes up in Minnesota. It was gruesome." Looking at the tank, she added, "I hope it hurts them like hell."

"I'll settle for quick."

"How will it affect other fish? If it's so dangerous, we could set off other fish kills."

"I picked this one exactly because it is so dangerous. We can't take any chances and yes, other fish will die. But VHS is decidedly deadly in lakes. The ocean is vast enough to dilute it and have as minimal impact as possible. It won't be pretty, but it can be effective."

Dhalia found them. She held a brown paper bag and tray with two large cups of coffee. Dressed in new clothes and smelling faintly like raspberries, she still looked like she hadn't slept much.

"Big day," she said, handing Suzanne the bag. "Bagels and cream cheese. I didn't know what kind you liked, so I got a half dozen to choose from."

Whit's stomach, hearing food was near, growled. He patted it down.

"You are a godsend," he said, tearing into a sesame bagel.

"I got a call on the way in," Dhalia said. "We're going to have a lot of high level visitors. They all want to hear what you have to say and see the results of your experiment."

"I'm ready for them," Whit said, brushing sesame seeds off his chest. "Has anyone spotted more chimaeras lurking around?"

"Just a few, though who knows what's too deep for us to see. The waters around Miami and miles out are off limits. I never thought I'd see martial law declared on the ocean."

"You'd have to be a madman to even want to go out there," Suzanne said.

"Someone did. Crazy guy with a GoPro and a jet ski," Dhalia said. "He was swallowed up pretty quick. He was streaming live, so whatever lunkhead was his partner already loaded it to YouTube. It's going viral. People are sick."

Whit shook his head. There was never a shortage of crackpots. More would come out of the woodwork if they didn't get a handle on this quickly.

He decided to go outside and wait for his special disease delivery.

Five hours later, there were too many people to fit in Dhalia's office, so they took things outside near the whale tank. Whit lost track of who was who, some men in tight-fitting military uniforms, others in plainclothes. He did his best to answer all their questions. They were angry, curious, concerned and some, even a tad frightened.

Suzanne bravely spoke up, positing her theory about where the chimaera fish came from and the relation to the melting of methane-laden ice. That really caused an uproar, which she and Whit did their best to quell.

"Believe it or not, we've seen it for ourselves," Whit said. "These fish haven't just been hiding for millennia and decided to come out now. We'll have more answered once we run a battery of tests. For now, my only concern is stopping them. And to that end, we're going to feed virus-laden cut bait to the two chimaera fish in this tank."

A white container of sliced up ballyhoo was wheeled in by Dhalia.

"The bait in here is loaded with the VHS virus. Think Ebola for fish. Despite their size and strength, I have reason to believe they have very weak immune systems. What could take weeks in a normal fish may just take hours."

Everyone was silent as the bucket was lifted over the tank by a pulley. It tipped over, spilling the hot fish parts. The chimaeras thrashed in the tank, eager to consume the fish. Several times, the tank hummed as the fish slammed into it. Several of the officious spectators took steps back.

"Now all we can do is sit back and wait," Whit said.

A large screen monitor had been set up so everyone could watch the camera feed. The fish had eaten everything, the water in the tank tinted pink. They swam in tight circles.

He overheard someone whisper, "This better work. If not, we're going to have to scour the Atlantic with every warship and submarine we have."

Whit hoped it didn't have to come to that, though he would need the Navy's help to finish the job that the VHS would start.

It only took an hour before the smaller chimaera began swimming erratically, trying to leap out of the tank. Its eyes bulged outward. There were traces of blood around its gills. It was working!

Thirty minutes later, the larger chimaera followed suit. Within two hours, both were dead.

Whit turned to everyone. "Let's talk about how we get this where it needs to go."

Going over his carefully considered plan, Whit felt Suzanne's hand slip into his. He caught her gaze and saw the pride she felt for him.

Pride and something more, something they'd once had and lost.

At least there was one good thing to come out of this.

TWENTY-EIGHT

It took a week to get everything in place.

A week of the waters around Florida devoid of anything but Navy ships on patrol, keeping the chimaera fish around by dumping barrels of chum into the Atlantic.

Keep your enemies closer.

They wanted as many of the prehistoric fish as possible in a controlled area. The chimaeras relentlessly attacked the destroyers and warships to no avail. Even they couldn't take down the mighty ships.

It had also been a week of funerals – five hundred and twenty-seven in all.

On Wednesday, Suzanne flew to Tom's hometown of Belmar, New Jersey to be there when he was laid to rest. He left behind his distraught, elderly parents. She wondered if either would see another year. They were that heartbroken.

Suzanne returned to Miami, determined to be front and center to see Whit's master plan through. Teams of scientists and bureaucrats kept Whit bouncing like a pinball night and day. They fought over the best way to contain and destroy the prehistoric killers, but in the end, Whit's approach was adopted. They all agreed not to release any details to the public. The last thing they needed was to awaken bleeding hearts that would cry out for the rights of the chimaera fish.

At one point, Suzanne thought, *I'm usually one of those bleeding hearts*. Not this time. She wanted them to pay for what they'd done, despite there never being any true intention in their actions. They were hardwired to be supreme predators.

After that, the biggest hurdle was getting enough of the VHS virus ready so it could be injected in the tons of cut bait. The Navy was calling it Operation Feeding Frenzy.

Several more chimaeras were captured alive and fed the VHS infected bait. So far, it had a one hundred percent mortality rate. Tests run on the plethora of dead chimaeras confirmed Whit's theory that their immune systems weren't capable of living long in this new world. But anything more than one day was too long.

Aside from the VHS, there was one more aspect of the chimaeras that would work to their advantage. They didn't go off on their own very much. Like any creatures with a hive mind, they stayed in clusters. The power and collective intelligence of a group far exceeded their capabilities when left on their own.

"That means they're even more dangerous," Suzanne said.

"In a manner of speaking, yes. But it also means we can address precise concentrations of chimaeras. Stragglers won't be much of an issue."

"So what do we do, herd them like cattle?"

Whit said, "Orca pods have been herded for decades so prime specimens can be captured for aquariums all over the world. It's barbaric to see children separated from their mothers. Once you hear their cries of desperation and anguish, you'll never look at them the same way again. It can be done with the chimaeras. We just need to give them a reason to swarm en masse."

"The way to a chimaera's heart is through its stomach," Suzanne said, regretting the slip of dark humor immediately. She shouldn't joke. Hundreds of families had been destroyed by the creatures.

Whit cocked an eyebrow at her. "And people say I'm the one with issues." His half-grin reassured her that he didn't think she was a monster. "But you're right. The cut fish will get some of them here, but we need to add a hell of a lot more to the stew to gather as many as we can in one place. We'll use their appetite against them."

That led to more meetings and frantic phone calls, some of them lasting well past midnight. Sixteen and twenty hour days, one after the other, were taking their toll on both of them.

She and Whit stayed in the same hotel, but rarely saw each other. He was the man of the hour, spending more time with military men the final two days than scientists because this was preparation for an all out war. They did meet for dinner one night, both too exhausted to say much, but happy to be in each other's company. He walked her to her room, and like a gentleman, kissed her cheek and said goodnight. She didn't know what was happening between them, but she couldn't lie to herself and say she wasn't curious.

A black SUV picked them up on Saturday. She spent the entire ride on the phone with her boss and her boss's bosses, reconfirming the data she'd compiled that was now in the Navy's hands. Whit's leg jittered non-stop. She placed a palm on his knee to calm him down. Powering her window down, she chain-smoked three cigarettes.

"I'll quit tomorrow," she said when she noticed Whit staring at her, waving the smoke away from his face.

"You're starting to sound like me," he said.

As promised, they stopped to get Shirley. Being part of Suzanne's original team, it was easy to have her upgraded to essential personnel. Simon had gone AWOL, presumably back home to Arkansas.

And now the three of them were on board a Navy destroyer, the *USS Farragut*, watching the sun come blazing to life over a purple sea.

The American military machine wasn't taking any chances this time around. Thanks to the media and the power of individually driven social media, the whole world had seen what the mass of chimaera fish could do, the savage destruction they wrought. Today was going to be the start of a fight to the death.

They were going to hit the chimaeras with everything they had. The VHS virus alone wasn't going to ensure swift mass extinction. The ocean was alive not just with the prehistoric fish, but aircraft carriers, destroyers, battles ships, amphibious assault ships and cruisers.

The air thrummed with the force of fighter jets tearing ass overhead. They made Suzanne's teeth tingle, her ribcage quake as they roared past. Everywhere they looked, there were F-14

Tomcats, Hornets and Harriers. All of them were armed to the teeth, the pilots assured they would come home empty.

Below the surface, out past the harbor, nuclear submarines kept a tight watch on the chimaeras lurking from sight. Those subs would play a very important part of the all out assault.

Not since World War II had such an awesome display of power been assembled in one place.

The world watched with keen interest. An endless stream of news vans lined the coast, all cameras trained on the Navy ships. After all, if the fish weren't stopped here, they could travel to international waters, laying waste to everything they came across.

Suzanne looked down and saw a chimaera leap up and slam itself benignly against the solid hull.

"No chance of them getting up here," she said.

"I just can't get over how damn ugly they are," Shirley said. She'd tamed her Mohawk, sweeping her hair to one side of her head. "You really like these things?"

Whit snorted. "*Like* is a strong word in this case. I've been fascinated by them. *Terrified* by this lot." An ear-splitting claxon sounded. "Come on, let's see how phase one is going."

Inside the bridge, everyone was focused on the reports coming over the radio.

Using Suzanne's coordinates for the methane vents, two Ohio-class Navy submarines were en route to assess and basically seal up the cracks.

"They're here all right," a calm, rock-steady voice said through the speakers. "Radar is crawling with them." This coming from the *USS New Mexico*, a nuclear submarine that she'd learned had been in active service for only a handful of years. It was one of modern warfare's most advanced defensive *and* offensive machines in the water today.

Suzanne nudged her way toward the commander, Captain Re. He looked too young to be in charge of the destroyer, but the thin wrinkles of crow's feet told her he was a little older than she'd initially thought. She'd seen him around during the planning phase and was always impressed by the questions he asked. He was a tough S.O.B., exactly what they needed. He'd welcomed them aboard an hour earlier, giving them full access to the ship but advising them to tread carefully, as men rushed about preparing for what was to come.

"Is that the main vent?" she asked.

Captain Re nodded, his jaw flexing. "Best to start from the top."

They could hear banging over the speaker.

"They're throwing themselves against the hull," the voice said.

"Hit it with what you got and get out of there," Captain Re commanded.

There was complete silence as they waited for the report back. Whit paced around the bridge.

Suzanne knew that the sub was deploying ballistic missiles to kill everything still living in the breach of the ocean floor, as well as to seal it shut. She worried about a sudden, deadly release of methane from the explosion, which is why there were no ships topside in the immediate area. Another destroyer was nearby, kitted up with instrumentation to read the methane levels to make sure all was safe.

"Well? Well?" Whit said.

"Give them a second," Suzanne said.

Not being able to see or hear anything was killing her, too. In a world where they had access to seemingly everything at the touch of a button, the silence was difficult to handle.

"Direct hit," the USS New Mexico reported.

A round of cheers erupted.

It was short-lived, as the second sub reported in from a lesser methane vent that they spotted chimaera fish as well. Guided missiles closed up shop while the USS New Mexico sped to the next destination. Both subs were taking a beating as the chimaeras, drawn to movement, went at them as if they were the last supper.

"How are the airborne methane levels?" Suzanne asked Captain Re.

He checked in and was given an all clear. Suzanne had been expecting the worst. She felt a small knot of tension at the back of her neck unwind. With the bombing, the ocean floor would be very unstable for days, if not weeks and months, to come. It would have to be closely monitored for methane and/or chimaeras.

Don't borrow tomorrow's worry, she admonished herself. They did exactly what they'd planned and hoped for today. Score one for the good guys.

"Bring them to us," Captain Re said to the captains of the destroyers and cruisers.

The idea was to have them act like Pied Pipers, leading the remaining chimaeras from their homes to the cordoned area off Miami. Massive containers of chum and infected cut bait slopped into the ocean as the destroyers and cruisers headed their way.

"We're going to have one hell of a welcome party for your fish," Captain Re said to Whit. He looked ready to protest, saying they weren't his fish for the hundredth time this week, but he held his tongue.

"It's working," Suzanne said.

"Don't get too excited yet," Whit said, dampening her spirits. "I just hope most of your other vents turn up empty. We might not have enough VHS to go around. I need these things dead, not dying slowly."

The next hour was spent listening in as the two subs visited each point in the map Suzanne had drawn out. One more vent had several chimaeras that didn't survive the blast. The next was devoid of the fish.

When the last two locations were declared clear, no chimaeras in sight, they braced themselves for phase two.

Whit stopped his pacing long enough to say to Suzanne and Shirley, "You sure you want to be here? I don't think it's too late to get you off the ship."

"Are you shitting me?" Shirley said. "I want a front row seat to see those bastards die. I can't have Danny back, but I can savor this moment."

Suzanne brushed a lock of hair from his eyes. "You got to be here to see my part of the plan. Now it's my turn to watch yours."

"And I can't thank you enough for all of your insight. You're smarter than I thought."

She gave his arm a solid punch. Whit gave an "Ouch!" and smiled.

"It's going to get ugly as hell," he said, rubbing the back of his neck.

"I was married to you for years. Ugly I can handle."

TWENTY-NINE

Whit's nerves hummed as if he'd stuck a fork in an electrical outlet.

The chimaera fish were being corralled in an area two miles wide. The water grew turbulent as more joined the party. Two destroyers and an aircraft carrier guarded the west, ready to obliterate any that tried to slip through. Beyond them, where Whit couldn't see, were now four nuclear subs as well as three warships and one battleship. It was a hell of a lot of firepower, but they needed it.

"I heard other countries have sent their best just to make sure the threat doesn't reach their own shores," he said to Suzanne. "They're out there, waiting to see if we succeed or fail."

There was a strong breeze, heavy with the musky odor of the giant chimaeras. They even *smelled* ancient.

"This is the first time I'm happy to hear that China has warships nearby," Shirley said.

In fact, a perimeter had been established right where the international waterline began, each quadrant filled with the deadliest ships over a dozen countries could provide. It was a risk, letting some of the United States' most powerful enemies so close to her shores. For once, they were all united against a common enemy. Ronald Reagan once posited that a threat from space would be the catalyst to bring nations at war together.

He was right. He just was just off on the direction of the threat.

A few passing seamen gave Shirley long looks.

"No crisis is too big for man to fall to his basic nature," Whit said.

"What?" Suzanne asked.

"Nothing. Just thinking out loud."

The *USS Farragut* had moved to the center of the maelstrom. The ocean foamed crimson as the cut bait was torn into by the frantic chimaera fish.

"This is the easy part," he warned them.

"Looks insane from here," Shirley said. The deck of the destroyer was a comfortable height from the ocean's turbid surface.

"What happens next?" Shirley asked.

"We wait for the VHS to consume their systems. If we got it right, it could take several hours. The smaller the chimaera, the quicker the effects. It's when they're in the throes of the infection that things can get dicey."

"What do you mean by dicey?" Shirley asked.

"Maybe frenetic is the right word. Just stay near the bridge."

The fish wailed against the *USS Farragut,* but the beast of a destroyer could weather their storm for months.

After all the planning, the amount of waiting the actual day brought was fraying Whit's patience.

This had to work.

Suzanne did her best to distract him but it was impossible latch on to her words long enough to make sense of them. He couldn't tear his eyes away from the churning water, chimaera fish packed in so tight, he could have walked on their backs to shore – provided they didn't eat him and he missed their venomous stingers.

"I haven't had a drink since that night we met up with you on the *Porpoise IV,*" he said, the thought coming from nowhere, or at least nowhere his conscious mind had been residing.

Suzanne was about to reply, the shock in her face either at the left field comment or the fact that he'd been bone dry for over a week, when several chimaeras exploded from the water, trailing blood that leaked from their distended eyes. They went higher than any chimaeras they'd witnessed so far. When they landed on their brethren's bodies, they convulsed on the waves.

"What the hell did you put in those bait fish?" Shirley said.

"A whole lot of very bad stuff," he said, moving toward the rail.

Two more fish made a tremendous leap to their left, then another to their right. It was like watching popcorn kernels at the bottom of a hot pan.

He looked toward the bridge. Captain Re stood at the window, observing the great displays of uncontrolled power.

"They supposed to react that way?" he called down to Whit through the loudspeaker.

He gave the captain a thumbs-up.

The fish, their nerves and organs on fire, blood vessels rupturing, were making a last desperate gasp to live, to outrun or outleap the disease that they couldn't know was killing them from the inside.

A chimaera fish with eyes that looked ready to burst from their sockets made it as high as the destroyer's deck. Machine guns tore it in half before it could wriggle its way aboard. The wind delivered a spray of blood out to sea.

Suzanne and Shirley moved closer to Whit.

"You weren't kidding," Suzanne said. "This is going to get ugly."

"I never kid when I'm murdering my lifelong obsession."

A claxon sounded again.

The ships began dropping depth charges. The VHS was the right punch to the jaw. The depth charges were a left to the gut.

Gouts of water and chimaera parts geysered all around them. The sound of the charges along with heavy artillery fire was deafening. The women covered their ears. Whit was too numb to think of protecting himself.

The all-clear was given to the circling fighter jets. Puffs of white smoke preceded the piercing whine of missiles as they shot into the boiling mass of chimaeras. The explosions vibrated through the massive steel ship, rattling Whit's bones from his feet to the plates of his skull. It sounded and felt like the hammer of God pounding damnation into the world.

It was tempting to run back into the bridge and curl up into a ball. His senses had never experienced anything like it, overloading his brain. He was like a primitive man, paralyzed by fear from a thunderstorm.

"Whit, look!" Suzanne shouted over the din.

An arrow formation of Tomcats dropped their payloads into the ocean. Thirty-foot gouts of water, blood and mottled flesh burst into the air. It reminded Whit a little bit of the fountains at the Bellagio Casino. These fountains would send people running for their lives, not taking pictures and video with their phones.

Whit moved closer to the edge of the ship, daring to look down.

He stumbled back as a pair of chimaeras went for him. They crashed against the deck, their heads almost squashing him. Whit pulled his legs up, rolling away as fast as he could. Men using handguns shot the fish as they slipped overboard.

"Oh shit, oh shit, oh shit," Whit stammered as Suzanne helped him to his feet.

The fish were making it onto the ships. It was as if the VHS had imbued their systems with supernatural strength, their death spasms making them even deadlier. The stench of cordite and gunpowder ran hard over the heady aroma of the infected creatures.

A chimaera made it fully aboard the *Farragut*. At maybe twelve feet long, it wove a path of destruction, snapping its jaws shut on two seamen while batting others aside as it jittered along the deck.

It was coming straight for them.

Whit tossed Suzanne toward the bridge. "Run!"

She wouldn't let go of his hand.

Someone's gun skittered by his feet. He picked it up.

"Just go!" he shouted.

Running at the chimaera, he shot at its eyes, actually hitting one. It exploded like a bag of jellied squid ink. A man was caught between its jaws, his body so compressed, some of his organs had bubbled from his mouth.

Warning blasts echoed between all of the Navy ships. More depth charges were released. Whit's chest ached from the repercussions.

The chimaera fish stopped thrashing, its body deflating, blood seeping from its gills.

The ocean was alive with the mad surge of dying chimaeras.

Some of the rocketing chimaeras were cut down in mid-flight by the fighter jets, their bodies sliced in half or in other cases, completely obliterated into a pink mist.

Wet drops spattered on the ship. It rained ocean water and chimaera fluids and viscera. The stench was ungodly.

A fresh wave of jets tore off the deck of the aircraft carrier, bringing more weapons to bear on the fish as they thrashed in the throes of a painful death. Looking to shore, even the media had been frightened off, taking leave of their prime positions. Whit guessed they figured they could cover the battle from a much further distance. They were smart to do it, and lucky that they had the option.

Gotta nut up, Whit, and see this to the end.

He just wondered how long the road would be to the end and if his nerves could last.

His head snapped around when he heard Shirley scream. Another chimaera had made it aboard. Shirley had fallen, her legs inches from its gaping, crimson maw.

Whit ran to her, the deck slick with ocean water and blood. He slipped, riding his knees until he grabbed her by the hand.

Using his forward momentum, he swept them both toward the fish but away from its mouth. Finding a dry patch of the deck, he brought them to their feet. They caromed against the fish, narrowly missing its venomous spine.

Sliding along its body, they fell again at its tail.

Shirley grabbed him by the cheeks and kissed him. "If we survive this, I'm calling you Dr. Jones from now on."

"But I'm not afraid of snakes," he said, relieved that he could still crack wise. It meant his mind wasn't totally off the reservation.

A couple of men came to their aid. "Get her inside," he barked.

Suzanne!

She was clutching one of the ladders leading to the bridge. When she saw him, she cried out with relief.

Everyone was moving for higher ground or the safety of the interior of the ship.

Whit urged Suzanne ahead of him, still holding the gun, keeping an eye on their backs.

Looking over the ocean, it was almost impossible now to see the chimaeras through the haze of smoke. Whatever ones made it on deck were strafed by men standing a level above. Those dying in the water were helped along by a steady diet of depth charges below and missiles from above.

He hoped someone was getting all of this, though video would never do it justice. It was like nothing man had ever seen. With hope, luck and prayer, there would never be anything like it again.

Whit held on to Suzanne and didn't let go. He watched the chimaeras die out, quickly and with more violence than the sea had ever seen.

At one point, his ears popped as if he were ascending in a plane. That was followed by ringing, then a hollow quasi-deafness that was most blessedly welcome. It was odd, seeing the intense battle between man and beast while hearing very little.

By nightfall, Captain Re placed an iron hand on his shoulder. "We're done here."

Whit's bones liquefied. He forced himself to stand upright.

"You sure?" he asked.

"I just got a quadruple confirmation. It's clear. Here. But we have an issue further out. Some have escaped. We need to corral the strays."

"Any estimates on how many we're dealing with?"

Suzanne's hand had slipped into his, mashing his knuckles together.

"A couple of hundred at the most. All of them top out on the larger end."

Whit sighed. "Of course. The bigger the chimaera, the longer it will take the VHS to shut down their systems."

"Can't we just let them go? They'll die anyway," Suzanne said. Her hand was cold and clammy. Beads of sweat dotted her pale forehead.

"No, we have to be sure," Whit said. "That's why we set up the safety net in the first place." Turning to Captain Re, he said, "Do I have a ride?"

The captain pointed at the silver helicopter hovering over the ship. "Door to door service."

Suzanne tugged his arm. "You don't have to go out there. Let the military finish this."

He cupped her cheek in his hand, noticing the specks of chimaera blood that covered them both. "This was all part of the plan. I need to…scratch that, I *want* to be there. I won't be able to rest until I see it end for myself."

"Then I'm going with you."

The Seahawk helicopter settled onto the bridge.

"Not this time," Whit said. "I won't be long." He hoped he was telling her the truth. "When this is done, we need to talk."

Tears rolled down her cheeks. She wasn't letting go of his hand.

"That's what I said to you when we broke up," she said.

He pushed a tear away with his thumb. "Yeah, well, I think it's time we put a positive spin on that particular phrase."

Captain Re walked him to the Seahawk. Whit couldn't look back. If he saw Suzanne, he knew he'd lose his nerve.

THIRTY

The interior of the Seahawk was so loud, everyone had to wear headsets. It sped close to the uneven ocean surface, racing to the their target. Whit's stomach had done so many backflips, he felt as if he'd swallowed a circus act.

"The good news is, they appear to be bunched into a pack," the pilot said in his headset. Whit could only see the back of his helmet. "And they're heading right where we want them to be."

In the distance, Whit saw the massive array of naval power, waiting to lay waste to the fleeing chimaeras.

"How many subs are out there?" he asked, pushing the small mic close to his mouth.

"Twenty-two."

Good. As reassuring as it was to see all of the material above the water, it was down below where it counted most, especially now that the fish had broken free and were on the run. They could dive too low for them to follow, scattering everywhere. Sure, the VHS would most likely kill them all in time.

Most likely.

Whit needed more than that. Shit, the world's oceans depended on it.

A dark hump broke through, foaming the water before disappearing.

A missile slammed into the spot a half-second later. The ocean boiled red. Two jets thundered on opposite sides of the Seahawk.

"Well, that's one less to worry about," Whit said.

The co-pilot gave him a thumbs-up.

"We just have to hope the rest are too weak and sick to fight or go much further," Whit said.

Neither man replied. Their job wasn't to speculate. They'd drawn the short straw, acting as high-end chauffeurs. He'd bet his paychecks for the next decade that they'd like to be the ones dropping holy hell on those monsters.

"Radar confirms they're within range," the pilot communicated to him. "Looks like the show is about to begin."

There were no more visible chimaeras. The rest had smartly chosen to dive deep down to familiar ground.

The water around the ships was alive with heavy splashes as a fresh round of depth charges were released. Whit could only imagine what it sounded like for the poor people stuck in those subs.

He worried about some suffering from friendly and not-so-friendly fire.

That's not your job. Better minds than yours must have taken that into account.

It did seem like the perfect situation for a hostile nation to accidentally take out an opponent's sub.

"You want us to open the channel?" the pilot asked.

"Yes, please," Whit replied. He had to hear the chatter between the various captains to see how everything progressed. He might be able to provide some insights into their behavior if things didn't go exactly according to plan.

It was a controlled mayhem of military jargon. He was calmed a bit by their matter-of-fact tones. The chimaeras were fully in their sights. More infected chum was spilled in an attempt to draw them up where there was more firepower.

"There they are!" Whit shouted.

Even in the throes of certain death, the chimaeras couldn't turn up a free meal. "I'd be just as hungry if I hadn't eaten for millions of years."

"What was that?" the co-pilot said.

"Nothing. Can we get any closer?"

He leaned forward, pointing to a writhing mass of chimaeras fighting over the chum. Missiles and machine gun fire zeroed in on them.

These chimaeras were enormous! They would make an orca turn tail and run.

"Just a little bit," the pilot answered. "Don't want to get in the line of fire."

"You and me both."

The water bulged as the underwater battle began, rolling humps of destruction. Whit wondered if each hump contained a chimaera body, dead or in bits. Despite all the horrors he'd witnessed, he still wanted to see. How can you know the boogeyman is dead if you don't get to view his corpse?

The Seahawk dipped. "This is as close as we get. It looks like…"

A chimaera shot out from the apex of one of the ocean bubbles. It was as if it had been blasted from an underwater cannon.

Its tail slammed into the side of the Seahawk, sending it into a violent spin. The cabin went wild with the sound of instrumental warnings.

Beep beep beep beep beep beep!

"Son of a fucking biscuit eater!" Whit wailed, reaching for the hand strap over his head. He clung for dear life while the pilots fought to regain control of the helicopter.

The Seahawk made a perilous dip, spun crazily, then magically pulled out of it.

The chimaera splashed back down, then made a beeline for the helicopter again. It was is if it could sense the Seahawk contained the architect of its demise and it wanted to take him with it into the cold, black nothing.

It missed. A screaming missile took its head clean off. The body slipped out of view, leaking all its fluids.

"Hold on!" the pilot shouted.

He'd managed to wrest control of the Seahawk, but only enough so it could make a hard landing on the ocean.

I'm going to die!

As someone who spent so much time in the ocean, Whit long suspected it would one day be the cause of his demise.

He just never pictured it like this.

The impact was so jarring, he almost blacked out. They may as well have landed on concrete.

"We have to get the hell out of here, now!" the pilot shouted, breaking the window with a pointed hammer. Ice cold water flooded the sinking helicopter.

Whit froze.

Would it be better to drown in the helicopter, or risk being eaten alive by a chimaera fish?

The co-pilot pulled him from his paralysis, dragging him through the busted window. The tread water as best they could in their waterlogged flight suits. Whit felt the bone-thrumming rumble of the explosive going off beneath them.

The ocean's chill set his teeth chattering immediately.

Please let hypothermia get us first!

The pilot spun around to say something to him. As he opened his mouth, he was suddenly tugged under.

"Wayne!" the co-pilot shouted.

Whit knew there was nothing they could do for him. Once a chimaera had you, death was the only way out. He sensed their deadly stingers all around him, massive jaws saving him for their last meal.

A massive chimaera appeared to their right. Its mouth opened wide, ready to suck them in.

Whit cringed when a missile ripped through its head. The chimaera misted before their eyes.

He looked up when he felt a strong draft wash over them. Another Seahawk hovered, dropping a line for them to cling to.

"Come on," he said to the co-pilot. "The cavalry's here!"

The end of the line had two harnesses. They quickly slipped into them. They were tugged upwards, the harness squeezing the air from Whit's lungs. He didn't care. He just wanted out of the damn ocean.

"Hurry up! Hurry up!" he urged their saviors with the little bit of breath he had. He kept looking back at the water, expecting a chimaera to grab them any second.

Instead, what he saw was an undulating tableau of death. Chunks of the mammoth chimaeras bobbed on the water.

The moment they were pulled into the helicopter, Whit asked, "How many are left? Any reports?"

The man covering them in shock blankets smiled.

"You're two lucky dogs. You go to be right there in the shit when the last one was taken out." He patted Whit on the shoulder. "Congratulations. "

Whit's vision wavered. He lay back, shivering.

He sure as hell didn't feel lucky.

THIRTY-ONE

Suzanne heard someone knocking on her door. Wrapped in a big terry cloth robe, she looked in the peephole before opening. Whit was on the other side, wearing one of the new shirts they'd picked out together, and a smile.

She opened the door, some of the steam from her shower escaping into the hallway.

"We're hired," he said, storming into the room and taking a seat by the window. He opened the shades to let in the morning sun.

Suzanne sat on the edge of the bed, putting her wet hair in a towel.

She said, "Hired for what? I already have a job."

"Not one that pays this much," he said. "They want us on for a year as consultants so they can sweep the ocean looking for signs of more chimaera fish. I told them we were a package deal. I'm talking mid six figures."

She tucked stray strands of hair under the towel. "Whit, that's your territory. I was only along for the ride because of their connection with the methane vents."

He rose from the chair. "Exactly. Even you said more and more methane is being released every year. If there are more chimaeras trapped under the ocean floor, you're our bloodhound."

Going to the mirror, she slapped his chest with the back of her hand. "Oh, so now I'm a dog that you need for your sea hunt. You know how to woo a lady."

Coming up behind her, he said, "I did at one time."

Suzanne felt his warm breath at the back of her neck.

"Besides, I don't think we're ready for a year of close quarters," she said.

"Not even if we got married on the beach in West Palm, followed by a second honeymoon at this little dive called Bora Bora?"

Her breath caught in her throat.

Was he being serious?

Turning to look him in the eye so she could ask him to repeat what he'd said, he kissed her.

"I even have a bottle of cold ginger ale outside waiting for us to celebrate," he said, scooping her into his arms.

Simon DiNardo worked the controls of a brand new, unmanned submersible. The scientific ship he was on, *Dennis T. Menace,* was anchored off Ireland's western coast.

This sub was a one-man operation, just the way he liked it. He hated sharing control with someone else. It was bad enough having to be told what to do.

No more working with climatologists for him. Or ichthyologists. That had almost gotten him killed.

Better to work for a telecommunication conglomerate, spot-checking the Trans-Atlantic Cable System. It was boring, but boring and a paycheck were the only things he wanted.

A hot ball of dread tightened in his gut when the sub's cameras came across a rising twister of tiny bubbles as it made its descent.

"You gotta be fucking kidding me," he grumbled.

"Something wrong?"

Simon kept his eyes on the monitor.

"Nothing. Just talking to myself."

As the submersible dropped further down, he thought he saw a flash of brown on the left corner of the screen. Whatever it was, it was fast.

And goddammit, it was big.

FIN

CHECK OUT OTHER GREAT
DEEP SEA THRILLERS

MEGA
by Jake Bible

There is something in the deep. Something large. Something hungry. Something prehistoric.

And Team Grendel must find it, fight it, and kill it.

Kinsey Thorne, the first female US Navy SEAL candidate has hit rock bottom. Having washed out of the Navy, she turned to every drink and drug she could get her hands on. Until her father and cousins, all ex-Navy SEALS themselves, offer her a way back into the life: as part of a private, elite combat Team being put together to find and hunt down an impossible monster in the Indian Ocean. Kinsey has a second chance, but can she live through it?

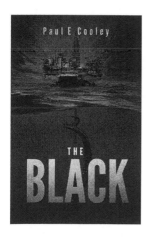

THE BLACK
by Paul E Cooley

Under 30,000 feet of water, the exploration rig Leaguer has discovered an oil field larger than Saudi Arabia, with oil so sweet and pure, nations would go to war for the rights to it. But as the team starts drilling exploration well after exploration well in their race to claim the sweet crude, a deep rumbling beneath the ocean floor shakes them all to their core. Something has been living in the oil and it's about to give birth to the greatest threat humanity has ever seen.

"The Black" is a techno/horror-thriller that puts the horror and action of movies such as Leviathan and The Thing right into readers' hands. Ocean exploration will never be the same."

CHECK OUT OTHER GREAT
DEEP SEA THRILLERS

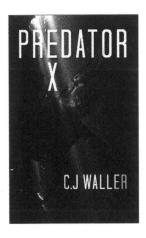

PREDATOR X
by C.J Waller

When deep level oil fracking uncovers a vast subterranean sea, a crack team of cavers and scientists are sent down to investigate. Upon their arrival, they disappear without a trace. A second team, including sedimentologist Dr Megan Stoker, are ordered to seek out Alpha Team and report back their findings. But Alpha team are nowhere to be found – instead, they are faced with something unexpected in the depths. Something ancient. Something huge. Something dangerous. Predator X

DEAD BAIT
by Tim Curran

A husband hell-bent on revenge hunts a Wereshark...A Russian mail order bride with a fishy secret...Crabs with a collective consciousness...A vampire who transforms into a Candiru...Zombie piranha...Bait that will have you crawling out of your skin and more. Drawing on horror, humor with a helping of dark fantasy and a touch of deviance, these 19 contemporary stories pay homage to the monsters that lurk in the murky waters of our imaginations. If you thought it was safe to go back in the water...Think Again!

CHECK OUT OTHER GREAT
DEEP SEA THRILLERS

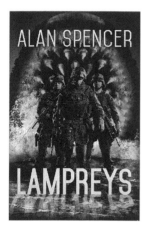

LAMPREYS
by Alan Spencer

A secret government tactical team is sent to perform a clean sweep of a private research installation. Horrible atrocities lurk within the abandoned corridors. Mutated sea creatures with insane killing abilities are waiting to suck the blood and meat from their prey.

Unemployed college professor Conrad Garfield is forced to assist and is soon separated from the team. Alone and afraid, Conrad must use his wits to battle mutated lampreys, infected scientists and go head-to-head with the biggest monstrosity of all.

Can Conrad survive, or will the deadly monsters suck the very life from his body?

DEEP DEVOTION
by M.C. Norris

Rising from the depths, a mind-bending monster unleashes a wave of terror across the American heartland. Kate Browning, a Kansas City EMT confronts her paralyzing fear of water when she traces the source of a deadly parasitic affliction to the Gulf of Mexico. Cooperating with a marine biologist, she travels to Florida in an effort to save the life of one very special patient, but the source of the epidemic happens to be the nest of a terrifying monster, one that last rose from the depths to annihilate the lost continent of Atlantis.

Leviathan, destroyer, devoted lifemate and parent, the abomination is not going to take the extermination of its brood well.

67339192R00094

Made in the USA
Middletown, DE
10 September 2019